TWIST IN TIME
"HISTORY'S MYSTERIES REVEALED"

BY BILL COATE

HISTORY PUBLISHING GROUP
FRESNO, CALIFORNIA

For more information address
History Publishing Group, Inc., 5588 N. Palm Avenue #112,
Fresno, CA 93705.
(559) 439-7258 or (888) 439-7258

History Publishing books may be purchased for educational,
business, or sales promotional use. For information please
contact: Marketing Department, History Publishing Group,
Inc. at the above address and phone numbers.

Cover Design ©
Suzanne Moles/Wattleweb Global Solutions

Book and Cover Layout
Gunter Copeland/History Publishing Group, Inc.

Printing
Quill Driver Books/World Dancer Press, Inc.

ISBN 0-9768252-0-1

THIS BOOK IS
DEDICATED
TO MY
FAMILY, FRIENDS,
MENTORS, COLLEAGUES
AND STUDENTS .
THANK YOU
FOR YOUR LOVE,
ENCOURAGEMENT
AND SUPPORT.

TABLE OF CONTENTS

TABLE OF CONTENTS

TABLE OF CONTENTS

TABLE OF CONTENTS

TABLE OF CONTENTS

INTRODUCTION

This book was born out of the conviction that the historian must mediate history, or he/she will become a luxury that society can ill afford.

While the author is not a scholar in the technical sense, he has been a historian for thirty-three years. He has earned a B.A. and an M.A. in history and has taught the discipline in public schools since 1972.

Over these past three decades, one thing has become abundantly clear to the writer. Although almost everyone has an inner love for the past, most of us cannot abide a steady diet of Master's theses or Doctoral dissertations, as pivotal as they may be.

What lies closest to our hearts are good narrative histories--stories well told. We long for poignant accounts of the past, written with a flair that holds our attention. We are not a nation of monograph readers, but we do love lively accounts of our yesterdays.

The impact of these simple truths hit the author with full force when he first began his career teaching U.S. history in junior high school. It took just a day or two to understand that if he was going to engage these young minds to any significant degree, he would have to become a good story teller. His teenage students were not about to sit still for dull lectures and meaningless assignments.

By the same token, when he later became an adjunct history instructor at the college level, things were not much different. His students at National University responded with enthusiasm to any attempt to lift them above the normally dry, dusty monologues by using animated accounts of the American pageant.

Then ten years ago, he was challenged by a local television station to use his storytelling techniques to engage a broader audience. They envisioned a short run of historical vignettes that would serve to add something different to the nightly news. It proved to be one of his most exciting experiences as a historian.

He dipped into his haversack of history for some stories that had just a bit of irony--a little twist--thus the name, "Twist in Time". The response was immediate and sustained. People called the station to express their approval of a history segment that was part of the nightly news. They further indicated appreciation for history lessons that came without ivory towered condescension. In short, our Twist in Time made them feel connected to history without their having to endure a lecture.

Weeks melted into months and months into years, and now here we are, a decade later, not only bringing our Twist in Time to a growing television audience, but inviting history lovers from across the country to join us as we explore the ironic touches of our American past in this written publication.

The reader will quickly see that no era of American history is immune from those strange twists of fate that shake us from our dogmatic slumbers and give us cause for reflection. From Jefferson, Adams, and Jackson to Amelia Earhart and Adolph Hitler, our stories cover the broad spectrum of our nation's political, social, and economic past.

It is our hope that readers will find our "Twists" both enjoyable and worthwhile.

Bill Coate
Madera, California

TWIST IN TIME
"HISTORY'S MYSTERIES REVEALED"

The Presidential Seal of the United States

Throughout the history of the United States, a handful of men have ascended to the Presidency without being elected to office. John Tyler, Millard Fillmore, Chester Arthur, and Gerald Ford, all occupied the White House without the consent of the governed.

This fact, however, has not kept our unelected Presidents out of the history books, with one noteworthy exception. In 1849, David Rice Atchinson became the 12th President of the United States, but today, hardly anyone remembers his name.

James Knox Polk had just finished a pivotal one term as President. Under his expansionist policies, the boundaries of the United States spread from the Atlantic to the Pacific, and Polk announced that he was satisfied. He would not seek a second term.

This set the stage for the election of 1848. The Whigs nominated "Old Rough and Ready," General Zachary Taylor, while the Democrats choose Lewis Cass. It really wasn't much of a contest. Taylor the hero of the Mexican/American War, won handily, and prepared to take over the reins of government in March, 1849. There were, however, just two small problems.

In the first place, March 4, 1849, Inauguration Day, fell

on a Sunday. In the second place, the President-Elect was a very religious man. As a strict Episcopalian, Taylor refused to conduct any business on Sunday, and that included being sworn in as President.

Therefore, at noon on March 4, 1849, the terms of office for James Knox Polk and his Vice President, George Dallas, ended without their successors taking the oath of office. America would have been without a President had it not been for the Constitutional provision that allowed the Speaker of the House to be elevated to the Presidency in the absence of a President or Vice-President. That is how David Rice Atchinson ascended to the Presidency at Noon on March 4, 1849.

Speaker Atchinson's Presidency lasted for just 24 hours. On Monday, March 5, 1849, General Taylor took the oath of office, and Atchinson quickly became a has-been. Was he saddened at having to give up the scepter of power? Apparently not. When asked what he did with the rare opportunity of being President for a day, Atchinson simply replied, "I went to bed."

Hamilton and Burr

The United States owes a great debt to Alexander Hamilton. As our first Secretary of the Treasury, his aggressive plans for putting the newly created United States on firm financial footing were brilliantly successful. If only he had been as assertive with a dueling pistol, he might have lived to a ripe old age.

The headstrong Hamilton was chosen by President George Washington in 1789 to solve a host of financial problems facing the young nation. Sometimes he had to step on the toes of his political adversaries, but he always did what he thought was right and was never deterred. That's why folks gave him at least an even chance when Vice-President Aaron Burr challenged Hamilton to a duel.

Burr was at the end of his term as Jefferson's Vice-President, and knowing that he would not be offered an encore, he decided to run for Governor of New York. Burr had the backing of most of the Federalists except Hamilton, who opposed the Vice-President vociferously. Soon criticism led to insults and Burr issued his challenge for satisfaction.

The two men and their seconds met on July 11, 1804, at Weehawken, New Jersey, across the Hudson River from New York City. Armed with pistols, they stepped off the required number of paces and turned to fire. Much to everyone's surprise, however, Hamilton stood holding his gun to his side. He contemptuously refused to fire while Burr took perfect aim.

The Vice-President fired and Hamilton fell, mortally wounded. Within hours he was dead, and the nation was mourning its first Secretary of the Treasury. Today most folks scratch their heads with wonder at such blatant disregard for self-preservation, but few know the real reason for Hamilton's refusal to fire. He didn't shoot because of the memory of a dead son.

You see, just two years earlier, almost to the day, Philip Hamilton, Alexander Hamilton's eldest son was killed in a duel on that very spot where his father now faced Burr, and from that day forward the Secretary vowed that he would never again fire a gun in anger. He had to show up when Burr challenged him; his honor was at stake, but he didn't have to shoot. With the image of his slain son haunting him, Alexander Hamilton chose principle over pride and lost his life.

Alvin C. York

Sergeant Alvin C. York was a national hero, but not just because of his unparalleled exploits on the battlefields of World War I. He also won his place in the hearts of his countrymen for his moral stature. No one ever doubted that Alvin was a man of God. He had made a solemn promise to his mother that he would never drink, smoke or chew. He promised her that he would always live an upright life, and he held to it.

It was because of this strict moral code that he had to wrestle with his conscience when the United States entered World War I. Before he could shoulder his rifle, he had to decide whether or not he could kill another human being. This dilemma kept him up day and night, until finally he decided on the side of patriotism and marched off to battle.

Had the war been fought just a couple of years earlier, however, York would have been spared those pangs of conscience. His mother could attest to that.

After reaching the third grade, Alvin had quit school to help his father eke out a meager existence on their rugged, little family farm. For a while he followed his mother's puritan guidance, but then he left home to work for the railroad. That was his undoing.

Alvin York learned to drink moonshine right along with the best of them. On weekends, he rarely drew a sober breath. Month after month, he would gamble his wages away. By his own admission, he stayed out late most every night and had his share of powerful fist fights without ever being whipped.

Then M.H. Russell came riding into those Tennessee mountains preaching the Gospel. Somehow Alvin York wound up at one of his meetings and was converted. Overnight Alvin York became a changed man. He became a devout Christian.

So Sergeant Alvin C. York, having disavowed his profligate life and armed with a deep and abiding faith in the Almighty, set out slaying the enemy in record numbers during World War I.

One has to wonder how things might have turned out if he had remained a drunk.

Amelia Earhart

In July 1937, a gallant and skillful pilot vanished over Howland Island in the Pacific. Her name was Amelia Earhart, perhaps the best known aviatrix in the history of flight. If her public thought that she was the epitome of determination, they ought to have seen her private side. The woman had ice-water running through her veins.

Earhart had only been flying for two years when she set an altitude record for women by soaring to 14,000 feet, and she did it in a little open-cockpit plane powered by a three-cylinder air-cooled engine. Later she became the first woman passenger to cross the Atlantic by plane, and in 1923 she made history by being the first woman to actually fly solo across the Atlantic. Then in 1931, she shocked the world by getting married. Would this be the end to America's dare devil darling? Would some man tame her? Not a chance. The same iron will that she exhibited in public also reigned in her private life.

Amelia's intended was George Palmer Putnam, and while they were waiting in his mother's home for the justice of the peace to arrive, the bride handed the groom a letter. In it, Amelia let George know just what she expected out of their marriage.

At the outset, Amelia, although she did love George, expressed some reluctance to marry. She was afraid that it would interfere with her own ambitions. "In our life together," she wrote, "I shall not hold you to any medieval code of faithfulness to me, nor shall I consider myself bound to you similarly. Please let us not interfere with each other's work or play. In this connection," she continued, "I may have to keep some place where I can go to be myself now and then, for I cannot guarantee to endure at all times the confinements of even an attractive cage." In closing, Amelia exacted what she called a cruel promise. "You must let me go in a year if we find no happiness together."

Nobody knows how Amelia's marriage to George Putnam really worked privately, but one suspects that she charted her own course in the air and on the ground. She always had and she always would. In public or in private, Amelia Earhart apparently loved her independence more than life itself.

General Benjamin F. Butler

Resistance to what Southerners called the War of Northern Aggression took many forms. In addition to armed conflict, the citizens of the South stood ready to show their contempt for the Union army in ways that were almost as vexatious as drawn swords, especially down in New Orleans.

By the summer of 1862, the Union Navy, under Admiral David G. Farragut had made possible the occupation of New Orleans by General Benjamin F. Butler, who in addition to holding the city, announced his determination to force its citizens to bend their knees to his occupying forces. Unfortunately for the general, that was easier said than done.

While Union soldiers were apparently safe to walk the streets of New Orleans, their flag could not go unattended. On June 7, 1862, one fellow by the name of Mumford decided to haul down the stars and stripes and cut the flag of the United States up into lapel stickers. This was too much for the General. He ordered Mumford executed.

If Butler thought, however, that a hanging would elicit better manners from the Confederates, he was mistaken. Now it was the women's turn. The Southern belles developed the habit of congregating on the hotel balconies dressed in all of their fineries. Whenever a Yankee soldier passed by, they would all whirl around and flirt out their skirts, causing one officer to comment that "Those women evidently know which end of them looks the best."

The greatest insult to northern dignity, however, was yet to come. On one occasion Admiral Farragut himself, while walking to a dinner engagement, passed beneath the balcony of a hotel. Suddenly he was drenched in a downpour from above. Several women had emptied the contents of the hotel's slop jars directly on the heads of the Admiral and his party.

Butler was livid and issued his famous General Order Number 28 which said that any female showing contempt for the United States, shall be held liable to be treated as a woman of the night.

Butler always claimed that General Order 28 put an end to such loathsome expressions of contempt, but it was also noted that while performing patrol duty, the Union soldiers did so from the middle of the streets. They no longer seemed willing to subject themselves to the possibility of a vengeance from above, which often reeked to high heaven.

President Andrew Jackson

President Andrew Jackson was known as "Old Hickory." He was as tough as nails, and when he set out to do something, it was usually accomplished. No one ever really doubted that he would someday fulfill his promise to represent the "common man" in the White House, but neither did anyone ever expect his constituency to respond as it did when he was finally elected.

Andrew Jackson's affinity for the common man probably stems from his early life. As a youth, "Mischievous" Andy displayed much more interest in brawling and cockfighting than in his scanty opportunities for reading and writing. His grammar was always rough-hewn, and his spelling was unique. On more than one occasion, he misspelled the same word two different ways in the same letter!

As a young adult, Jackson lived by the dictum of the common man, "Give no insult, and take none." In one of his many brawls, the soon-to-be President of the United States bit the ear off of one of his opponents. There was no doubt about it, Andrew Jackson was made of the stuff the common man admired.

Then came the election of 1828. Jackson's opponent was the crusty, imperious, New England Puritan, John Quincy Adams. It was hardly a contest. The common man prevailed, and Jackson prepared to go to the White House, but on the way a funny thing happened.

On Inauguration day, "Hickoryites" poured into Washington, and characteristically, Jackson embraced them. A milling crowd of clerks, shopkeepers, hobnailed artisans, and grimy laborers were invited to the White House after the ceremony. When Jackson ordered the doors opened to the mob, they surged in, wrecking the china, climbing with muddy boots on the furniture, and threatening their hero with cracked ribs.

To lure Jackson's exuberant supporters out of the White House, tubs of lemonade and whiskey were set out on the front lawn. This of course did the trick, and the doors were quickly locked.

As for Jackson, he was spirited out a side door, and ironically spent his first night as President in a hotel room, thanks to the advent of the age of the common man.

Benjamin Franklin

Benjamin Franklin, was one of the most astute Americans of his time, and as such, he wasn't about to allow himself to be played like a violin. He was never known to yield to manipulation. At least that became the opinion of folks in Wrentham Massachusetts, after he turned them down on their appeal for help in obtaining a church bell.

The trouble began at the end of the War for Independence when a dispute arose which divided the citizens of Wrentham. The discord grew so intense that the dissidents departed, started their own town, and named it New Wrentham.

The first building the citizens set out to erect was their own church. This was not surprising since New England tradition put that institution at the cultural, social, religious, and governmental center of every town. The founding fathers of the new community went right to work, but there was a problem. When they finished building the church, someone noted that there was no bell in the steeple.

This meant that there was no way to summon the local citizens for services, or for emergencies such as fire. Therefore, the town leaders put their heads together and came up with a plan.

Knowing of Franklin's interest in community building, the folks of New Wrentham figured they could count on him for their bell. All they needed was to gain the old patriot's attention. To accomplish this, they put a proverbial carrot at the end of the stick and announced that they had changed the name of their town to Franklin, in hopes that he would help them.

Next they wrote him a letter, informing him of their action and asking him to donate a bell for their church. Dr. Franklin, however, was not too impressed. He wrote back, suggesting that "sense is better than sound," and offered a better way for him to assist the fledgling community.

Instead of a bell, Franklin sent the good citizens a crate of books, intimating that they should forget about the house of worship for awhile and start a library. For Franklin, books were much more important than the sound of a church bell.

The people followed Franklin's advice and as a result, today, over 200 years later, they have the oldest public library in the United States--a continuing monument to Benjamin Franklin's refusal to allow any group of people to use him for their own purposes, not even when they were willing to change the name of their town.

The Battle of New Orleans

The date was January 8th, 1815, and the British army had assembled eight thousand battle-seasoned troops on the outskirts of New Orleans. They were facing a hodge-podge force of Americans led by Andrew Jackson. The British sacrificed two thousand men that day, but by a quirk of fate, it was all so unnecessary.

The War of 1812 easily ranks as America's worst-fought war. The disunited country couldn't even defend its own capital, as the British put Washington D.C. to the torch and ran President James Madison into the nearby hills.

It is not surprising then that the British became a bit overconfident as they assembled just below New Orleans to attack the motley crew which General Andrew Jackson called his army.

On January 8, 1815, Sir Edward Pakenham led his redcoats in a frontal attack against the Americans. Awaiting his adversary's advance was Jackson with a polyglot collection of Tennesseans, Kentuckians, Creoles, and pirates drawn up behind breastworks. For all their drill and bravery, the lobster backs advancing through the open were no match for Jackson's well-protected men. Making good use of artillery as well as rifles, the Americans held their fire as each wave of attackers approached, then sent deadly volleys at close range. Finally the British retreated while an American band struck up "Hail Columbia" and sang this popular little ditty, "Behind it stood our little force--None wished it to be greater; For every man was half a horse, and half an alligator."

Left behind were seven hundred dead, including Pakenham himself, fourteen hundred wounded, and five hundred prisoners. Jackson's losses were confined to eight killed and thirteen wounded. Clearly the British lion's tail had been twisted, but it had all been for naught.

Two weeks earlier, on December 24, 1814, the peace treaty between the United States and Great Britain had been signed. The opposing forces in the Battle of New Orleans had no idea that the war of 1812 was over before that first shot was ever fired.

Benjamin Franklin

Everybody knows that Benjamin Franklin left this nation quite a legacy. His inventions, his diplomacy, and his plain old common sense are still admired today. There was, however, one bequest that wasn't appreciated by all of Franklin's contemporaries, and it landed his grandson in jail.

As he approached the end of his long life, Benjamin Franklin sat down to write his last will and testament. He all but passed over his son, William, not because he was illegitimate, but because the younger Franklin and his father were on opposite sides during the War for Independence and became bitter enemies.

Instead, Benjamin bequeathed almost his entire estate to his daughter Sara Bache, and to her son, Benjamin Bache, Franklin left his printing press.

Benjamin Franklin Bache, the grandson of Benjamin Franklin took possession of the press at the death of his grandfather. He started his own newspaper, and by the late 1790s he had become well known for his caustic commentaries about the administration of President John Adams.

That would have been all well and good, except that it was against the law. In 1798, Congress had passed the Alien and Sedition Acts which, among other things, made it a crime to criticize the government in print.

It should have come as no surprise that the grandson of Benjamin Franklin would not be throttled by this egregious attack upon the freedom of the press. He immediately began to publicly attack the administration's foreign and domestic policies. This, of course brought Bache into direct violation of the Sedition Act, and he was thrown into prison.

Two years later, Thomas Jefferson replaced Adams as President, and he pardoned all those convicted under the Sedition Act. Sadly, this did not free Bache from prison. He had died behind bars just a few months before. Apparently the grandson of Benjamin Franklin had inherited from his grandfather, not only the means to propagate great ideas, but the will to stand by them as well.

Boston Massacre

The snowball fight of March 5, 1770, is a well known story. British soldiers guarding the Boston custom house fired into an unruly mob of dock workers, killing five of them. When Samuel Adams, published an account of the shootings, the episode became known as the Boston Massacre. Little did the Patriot leader know the strange chain of events that would follow his expose.

After Sam Adam's publication, the colonists were furious and demanded justice. So vociferous were they, that the British authorities decided to make scapegoats of the Redcoats.

The first to be put on trial was Captain Thomas Preston. He was found innocent. That left the eight soldiers, who now realized more than ever that they needed a good lawyer. Had their Captain been found guilty, that would have rendered them guiltless; they had just been following orders. But with Preston having been found innocent, the soldiers were now on their own--hung out to dry. At that point, the best lawyer in Boston stepped in to take their case and save their lives.

When the trial opened, the defense attorney, who was himself a colonial, was held in almost as much ridicule as the soldiers. Cold stares surveyed him in court, and he met with outright hostility on the street. Nevertheless, he persevered.

The defense counsel maintained that the mob into which the defendants had shot, was in reality an unlawful assembly. So brilliantly did he argue the case that, after 2 1/2 hours, the jury came back with a not guilty verdict for six of the soldiers and manslaughter verdicts for the other two.

None of the defendants in the Boston Massacre went to jail. Even the two guilty ones, claiming a common law custom, escaped prison by being branded.

Thus it was that eight British Redcoats owed their lives and their freedom to a colonial lawyer who laid aside his own political feelings to do his duty. For you see, that Boston attorney who successfully defended the soldiers of the Boston Massacre was none other than John Adams, our second President, one of the most ardent anti-British patriots Massachusetts ever produced.

The McClean House at Bull Run

The American Civil War was a watershed in our nation's history. It redefined the character of the United States and sent the population of the South reeling, especially people like Wilmer McClean who always seemed to be in the wrong place at the wrong time.

Wilmer McClean was one of the more prosperous residents of Manassas Junction, Virginia, in July of 1861, when the Northern and Southern armies began to gather around his place. His 1,400 acre plantation straddled Bull Run, so the Confederates occupied his house and used it as its headquarters in this, the first real, full-fledged battle of the Civil War.

After the First Battle of Bull Run, McClean sold his farm and moved further west, out of the line of fire between the two contending armies. He assured his family, "the sounds of battle would never again reach them" in their new home.

In the meantime, battle followed battle. Chancellorsville,

Fredericksburg, Gettysburg, Vicksburg, and hundreds of others. For four years Billy Yank and Johnny Reb pounded each other, and as they did, they got closer and closer to Wilmer McClean's new home.

Finally in April, of 1865, Lee's Army of Northern Virginia and Grant's Army of the Potomac faced each other, and where do you think they were? Somehow the center of this horrific conflict, which began at his Bull Run farm four years earlier, had sought McClean out and found him once more. The Union and Rebel forces were camped once again, almost in his front yard.

On April 9, 1865, General Robert E. Lee surrendered to Ulysses S. Grant, and since they were so close, the combatants took over McClean's home once again--to agree upon and sign the terms of the capitulation. When he left his home on Bull Run to find that safe haven from the ravages of war, McClean settled near Appomattox Courthouse never dreaming that he was jumping from the frying pan into the fire.

The McClean House at Appomattox

Layfayette "Punch" Choisser

Back in the rough and tumble days of the Old West, not every lawman was as pure as the driven snow. Some of them had a long rap sheet and were hired simply to preserve the peace because of their prowess with a pistol.

Layfayette Choisser was one of these. After a life of crime and a stretch in the penitentiary, he was hired in Mariposa, California, to put his gun to good use, but alas, in the end he was unable to escape his unsavory past.

Choisser came to Bear Valley, near Mariposa, during the gold rush. Right away he drifted into bad company, spending most of his time in saloons and gambling halls, in and out of trouble.

Things came to a head on the night of October 29, 1857, when Choisser decided to have a drink in Joseph Bigler's saloon. He became inebriated and began to quarrel with Bigler. The saloon man resorted to fisticuffs and Choisser pulled his pistol. He shot Bigler only once, but that was enough. The barkeep fell to the floor and was dead in 20 minutes.

Choisser was convicted of manslaughter and spent five years in San Quentin. Although he was never arrested again, after his release, Layfayette's reputation as a tough gunslinger grew larger--so large that Sheriff John C. Clark sought him out as a deputy.

Choisser accepted, and for a while it looked as if he would escape his sordid past. He married, fathered a son, and became a powerful force for law and order. Then fate stepped in.

No one knows exactly how it happened or who did it. What is known is that on November 17, 1884, Choisser's horse returned riderless to his Bear Valley home. When his son went out to investigate, he found his father's body in the nearby Merced River with two large gashes in his head.

Strangely enough one Maurice Newman, the second husband of Margaret Bigler, the widow of the saloon keeper Choisser had shot and killed in 1857, was on the scene. He volunteered to ride to town for a doctor. It was of course too late.

Folks always wondered about Newman's presence at the murder site that night, but nothing more than rumor ever came of it. Everyone seemed content to allow the dust from the past to settle peacefully.

So they buried Layfayette Choisser with the pistol that couldn't save him. He had made a valiant effort to put it to good use, but it was a futile effort. He just couldn't seem to escape that old adage that "those who live by the sword die by the sword."

Brooks Assaulting Charles Sumner

Members of the Congress of the United States have a number of privileges, not the least of which is the right to say just about whatever they please on the floor of the Senate or the House. They can't be sued, and historically there has been little to restrain their rhetoric, except for that time when terseness was forced on one Senator with a club.

Charles Sumner came to the Senate from Massachusetts just before the Civil War. He was what we would today call a "dandy." Brilliant, learned, handsome, articulate, he had made a name for himself as a reformer, especially an anti-slavery reformer.

In the spring of 1856, Sumner, believing he could launch into a tirade with complete abandon, took a nasty swipe at the proponents of slavery, and in doing so made some vicious attacks on Senators Stephen A. Douglas and Andrew P. Butler. Although Butler was absent, Douglas heard it all and muttered, "That darned fool is going to get himself killed by some other darned fool." Indeed, that "fool" materialized in the person of Congressman Preston Brooks, a nephew of Senator Butler.

For a few hours, Brooks thought about challenging Sumner to a duel. Then he decided that he could reflect his contempt more effectively with a cane. Two days after Sumner made his comments from what he thought was the safe harbor of the Senate floor, Congressman Brooks entered the chambers as it adjourned. While Sumner remained at his desk writing, Brooks approached his kinsman's critic, cane in hand.

Before anyone knew what was happening, Brooks was raining blows down upon the head of Senator Sumner, who fell to the floor "bellowing like a calf."

As disreputable as it was, Brooks showed that no one spoke with complete immunity on the floor of Congress. That caning took Charles Sumner out of the Senate and shut him up for three years.

And it made no difference that the House censured Brooks. He resigned, returned home, and was triumphantly reelected. In the meantime the representatives of the people learned a lesson; freedom of speech is not absolute and certainly not without its consequences--not even on the floor of the United States Senate.

George Armstrong Custer at Little Big Horn

It was the discovery of gold in the Black Hills that set the stage for the last stand of George Armstrong Custer. Thousands of miners invaded the land that had been occupied by Native Americans since time immemorial, and a severe culture clash ensued.

By the summer of 1876, an army of troops under the

command of General Alfred H. Terry, had been sent to answer the threats from several tribes who had concentrated in the region of the Big Horn River. Terry dispatched Custer to block the Indians' escape route into the Big Horn Mountains.

The vain and rash Custer took 304 men with him, and the history books tell us that they all perished. A closer look, however, reveals that some of Custer's men didn't die. Forty of them survived simply because the Colonel made them mad.

The foolhardy Custer set out for the Little Big Horn accompanied by thirty Arikaras, six Crow, and four Sioux Indians whom he had hired as scouts. After a quick reconnoiter, they informed Custer that he was hopelessly outnumbered and strongly urged that he wait for reinforcements.

Custer, however, always the headline seeker, did not want to share his presumed glory with anyone else and insisted on pressing forward with the attack. At that point, one of the Crow scouts shed his uniform saying that since he was going to meet the Great Spirit, he wanted to be dressed as an Indian, not a white man. An enraged Custer fired all of his Indian scouts and ordered the 264 remaining troopers forward.

When he reached the Little Big Horn, Custer ran into 2,500 Sioux led by Sitting Bull, Crazy Horse, and Rain-in-the-Face. He and his men fought bravely, but every one of them died on the spot.

We don't know what happened to Custer's Indian scouts, but one thing is for sure. They didn't die with him, although they apparently were willing to do so. In the end, their lives were saved by Custer's temper tantrum. Born of an over-zealous and reckless nature, the Colonel's cocksure attitude removed his Native American scouts from the battle. Had he been turned differently, there might have been forty more bodies to bury as a result of Custer's Last Stand.

Colonel Elmer Ellsworth

Symbols! They can make one swell with pride or wretch in disgust. Take that flap about flying the Confederate flag above the state house in South Carolina for instance. That may have been the most recent fight over that symbol, but it won't be the last, and it certainly wasn't the first.

The guns had barely quieted at Fort Sumter when President Lincoln ordered that Alexandria, Virginia, just across the Potomac, be taken from Rebel hands. After all, there staring him in the face each morning was the Confederate flag flying from atop the Marshall House, and he wanted it taken down.

The soldier who was placed in charge of this detail was Colonel Elmer Ellsworth, one of the four soldiers who formed the President's body guard. Ellsworth's orders were simple. Take the town and remove that flag. The former was easy, but the latter had its price.

Ellsworth's troops landed early on the morning of May 24, 1861. There was no resistance, so the Colonel marched directly to the Marshall House where the offending bit of bunting waved in the breeze. Flanked by a quartet of soldiers, Ellsworth climbed to the second story of the hotel unmolested.

From one of the top windows he clambered out onto the roof and cut the flag from its staff. With the emblem in hand, Ellsworth then made his way back to the stairs from which he intended to descend and make secure his occupation of Alexandria.

He had no more than reached the top step when from out of the shadows lurched an enraged Rebel who would not stand for such an abominable sacrilege as the desecration of the Confederate flag. He raised a gun to Ellsworth's heart and fired, killing him instantly. Needless to say the assassin was quickly dispatched as well.

They brought Ellsworth to Washington where Lincoln mourned the fallen soldier calling him the "greatest little man I ever met." In the meantime, the Confederate flag never went back up on the Marshall House, but it flew in thousands of other places, and as recent events show, it still stirs the emotions of partisans, almost 140 years after that first forced removal of the stars and bars.

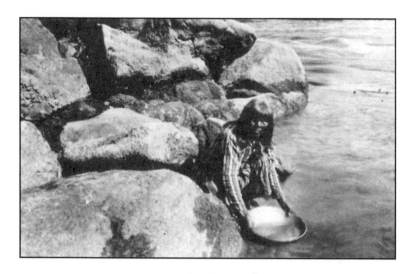

Chukchansi Indian Panning for Gold

Gold! Placer gold! Rock-bound gold! Gold in all of its varied forms. News of its discovery spread like a wild fire fanned by the wind. The very thought of it made hearts beat and bosoms sigh. That's what powered the California gold rush, and that's what brought miners with a frenzy in their souls to the gold fields.

Among the many placer bearing streams that coursed down the western slopes of the Sierra Nevada was Coarsegold Creek, a tributary of the Fresno River. Gold--heavy, coarse gold--was discovered in abundance along that gulch. With miners probing for placers on every creek and stream of the southern Mother Lode, it is no surprise that this entire area was inundated quickly with picks, pans, and prospectors who were all infected with gold fever.

Some have estimated as many as 10,000 souls rushed to the area when word of the discovery leaked out in 1850. Most of the miners were concentrated in the Texas Flat area, just a mile or two west of the little, present-day town of Coarsegold. It was root hog or die as the argonauts took possession of the land, ignoring the fact that it had been the ancestral home of the Chukchansi Indians for centuries.

The Native Americans didn't take the invasion lying down. They fought for their land, but in the end had to submit to superior firepower and retreated to the hinterland to maintain their tribal identity. In the meantime the town of Coarsegold popped up along the creek. For years it was a sleepy little mountain village, secure in its future and its past. It was known as the town that gold created.

Now, however, another kind of rush for gold is forming and promises to overshadow Coarsegold's 19th century pioneer image. Years from now, historians will point to Indian gaming and the opening of the Chukchansi Gold Casino as a watershed in the history of Coarsegold. It will be written that those early miners who, in their frantic search for gold, shoved the Indians aside, were themselves upstaged by descendants of the Native Americans they tried so hard to displace.

By building gambling casinos on their land, the Native Americans are getting the gold after all. History, it seems, is just full of sudden, strange twists and turns.

President Calvin Coolidge

On August 6th, 1923, Warren G. Harding died suddenly at the age of 57, and with his passing, Vice-President Calvin Coolidge ascended to the Presidency. The nation's new chief executive was something of an enigma, but he wanted it that way. Folks didn't call him "Silent Cal" for nothing.

It didn't take long for the taciturn Coolidge to win a place in the hearts of the American people with his wry wit and calm manner. In fact the nation developed something of a love affair with his pithy one-liners.

His most famous, of course, was his dictum that the "business of America is business," but second to that was an exchange he had one evening at a White House function. The President had invited the press corps to a social event, and one rather pushy reporter attempted to set Coolidge up for an interrogation. She informed Silent Cal that before coming to Washington, she had made a bet. She told the President that she had wagered she could engage him in a conversation which would consist of more than his usual yes and no responses. In fact, she told Coolidge that she had bet she could engage him in at least a three word conversation. The President eyed his young guest, leaned over, and gently replied, "You lose."

Then there was that time when someone woke him up from his customary afternoon nap. The blurry eyed President sat up, looked around and asked, "What's wrong? Isn't the country still here?"

Now the reasons given for Coolidge's terse eloquence are many, but it's best summed up by the man himself. On December 6, 1923, just prior to making the very first Presidential radio broadcast to the nation, and aware that he possessed a rather sober personality, he said, and we quote, "The American people seem to want a solemn ass as a President, and I think I'll go along with them." And that's just what Calvin Coolidge did.

With all the political hot air that's being passed around now, it's enough to make one yearn for those good old days when terseness was almost a virtue.

Thomas W. Custer, Boston Custer, Lt.James Calhoun

The Battle of the Little Bighorn--June 25, 1876--
Some remember it as Custer's Last Stand, for it was on that
day that the flamboyant Lt. Colonel George Armstrong Custer
made a mistake that cost him dearly, and not only him but his
entire family.

In late 1875, with the continued intrusions of Whites
into their sacred lands in the Black Hills, hundreds of Sioux
and Cheyenne Indians left their reservations with the great
warrior Sitting Bull, to fight for their territory.

To force the Indians back on the reservations, the army
dispatched three units. One of these included Custer and his
Seventh Cavalry, which by June 1876, had managed to come
upon a huge number of warriors on the Little Bighorn River.

In what was a disastrous error of judgment, Custer

split his own force in three parts. One column under Captain Frederick Benteen was sent to block an escape route through the upper valley of the river. Another column under Major Marcus Reno was sent to pursue a group of Indians across the river, while Custer led the remaining 210 troopers to attack the village. Suddenly they found themselves cut off from the rest of his force and completely encircled by Indian warriors.

Every man fighting with Custer died that day. The army had to notify the families of the 210 soldiers who lost their lives, and Custer's was particularly hard hit, for not only did the brash, headline seeking officer die, two of his brothers and his brother-in-law went down with him.

Riding with George Armstrong Custer on that day were his brothers Thomas W. Custer, recipient of two Congressional Medals of Honor during the Civil War and commander of Company C of the 7th Cavalry and 28 year old Boston Custer who was a guide and teamster for the regiment. Also riding with the Custers was their brother-in-law, Lt. James Calhoun who had married their sister Margaret Custer.

After the battle was over and retribution taken on the remains of the soldiers, they were buried where they fell. Later, however, George Armstrong Custer, Thomas Custer, Boston Custer and Lt. Calhoun. were disinterred and reburied in other cemeteries back east.

It seems that they shared as much in death as they did in life. One could even make the case that, for the Custers, fighting Indians was a family affair.

Johnny Clem

In 1932, a dottering old man dressed in an old army uniform asked for quiet. A crowd of well-wishers had gathered to celebrate his 80th birthday. Everybody present, including the press, referred to him as Major John L. Clem, but he wanted to be remembered as "The Drummer Boy of Shiloh."

Johnny Clem was one of the youngest soldiers of the Civil War. He was just ten years old when he served as a drummer boy for the 22nd Michigan Infantry.

The soldiers of Johnny's unit saw a little action in 1861, but it wasn't until the Battle of Shiloh in early April of 1862, that they received their baptism by fire, and it just so happened that the young drummer boy got caught right in the middle.

On April 6, Johnny's unit was caught off guard and was almost pushed into the Tennessee River. During the fighting a Union soldier dropped right at his feet, nailed by a sharpshooter. Ten year-old Johnny picked up the dead man's rifle and drew a bead on a Rebel Colonel who had failed to see the small lad with the big gun. In the next instant, the Confederate officer was on the ground. Johnny Clem had killed him with one shot.

The Battle of Shiloh lasted two days and up to that time was the bloodiest conflagration that had ever been fought on the American continent. The North lost 13,000 men, while the South counted 10,700 casualties.

An account of the Battle of Shiloh of course made the newspapers, and in every piece, the story of Johnny Clem's bravery was told. Soon the entire nation knew about him.

Johnny ended the war as a teenage Sergeant and sported a medal given to him by the Secretary of the Treasury. He remained in the army and retired at the age of 65 with the rank of Major. When Clem died at the age of 82, his military tombstone was inscribed with the usual information: name, regiment, company and state, but in Johnny's case it also carried an epitaph, "Here lies the Drummer Boy of Shiloh." Now no one would forget.

John Rowlands

One of the most peculiar aspects of the Civil War era is the fact that its landscape was crowded with figures who were marked for later fame. Generally, these individuals were cast in minor roles in the conflict itself, but they certainly made their entrances on the stage of world history in the years that followed. Take Private John Rowlands, for instance.

Rowlands was a member of the 6th Arkansas Infantry. He was just twenty years old on that April Sunday in 1862, which could help explain his actions during the bloody battle of Shiloh.

Confederate infantrymen stormed the last center of Federal resistance on the first day of the battle, and Rowlands was there. He had come up from Cypress Bend with the "Dixie

Greys." When the darkness silenced the musket fire, Rowlands and his Confederate comrades were much relieved. On the next day, however, it was a different story. The Northern army regrouped and pushed back. In the confusion that followed, Rowlands was captured.

As he was about to be herded back to a Yankee prison, Private Rowlands had a sudden change of heart. He indicated that he now realized that he had been on the wrong side all along. He wanted to switch sides and join the Union Army! And that's what he did.

It wasn't long, however, before marching under the Union blue got the best of Rowlands, so he reported himself ill and was dismissed on account of poor health. Now he was faced with a dilemma. He couldn't remain with the army, and he couldn't go home, so he came up with another idea. He joined the Union Navy.

Rowlands served in the Navy until the end of the War, and when he wasn't immediately discharged, he deserted that branch of the service.

All told, his was a pretty dismal service record. He had been a turncoat, a malingerer, and a deserter. Maybe that's what later propelled him to action in a far off continent--Africa. For you see, in time John Rowlands changed his name to Henry M. Stanley, and it was he, this failure as a soldier and a sailor, who searched for and found Dr. David Livingstone in 1871, and uttered that now famous line, "Dr. Livingstone, I presume?" Who would have ever guessed?

Warren G. Harding

Today's elections, it seems, cannot be conducted without spasms of vigorous mudslinging. Nearly everybody complains about the negative campaign tactics that always manage to cloud the issues. It's enough to make the modern voter cast a jaundiced eye toward the system--until one considers the past.

Personal attacks in political campaigns are nothing new. History has recorded some vitriolic exchanges that would make today's public disparagements sound almost genteel. Consider for a moment the campaign of 1860. Four candidates had their hats in the ring: Abraham Lincoln, Stephen A. Douglas, John Bell, and John C. Breckinridge. The four men fought like cats and dogs, and the campaign reached its nadir when Lincoln's opponents began to make fun of his looks. Lincoln's handlers rejoined by asserting, "We know Old Abe does not look very handsome, but if all the ugly men in the U.S. vote for him, he will surely be elected."

Then there was the election of 1884. Grover Cleveland was running against James G. Blaine, but he had a problem, and the Blaine people took full advantage of it. Cleveland was the father of a child born out of wedlock. Blaine said that he didn't believe that voters would "knowingly elect to the Presidency a coarse debauchee who would bring his harlots with him to Washington.

Now if that isn't enough, let's go to 1920 when Warren G. Harding was running against James Cox and Eugene Debs. This time it was the Socialist candidate who got off the best zinger of the campaign. Never known for his intellectual depth, Harding was accused by Debs of being stupid. His opponent, Debs charged, discussed the issues by "uttering pompous phrases that moved over the landscape in search of an idea."

It was the election of 1936, however, that brought out the worst in the political operatives. Stunned by Franklin Roosevelt's victory four years earlier, Alf Landon's campaign manager was quoted as saying that "If the President became convinced on Tuesday that coming out for cannibalism would get him the votes he needed, he would begin fattening a missionary in the White House backyard come Wednesday."

So the next time that civility seems to be slipping away from our political process, it might help to remember that our forefathers weren't the most magnanimous campaigners who ever hit the trail.

Edmund Ruffin

The Confederate States of America had no more fervent advocate than Edmund Ruffin. The man was loyal to the bone. So widely known was his patriotism that he was given the honor of firing the first shot of the Civil War, never dreaming that he was lighting the fuse of his own demise.

If Southern thought and action could be represented in a single individual, then Edmund Ruffin would be the most likely candidate. Born in the early days of the Republic, Ruffin was a Virginia farmer whose experiments in soil chemistry markedly improved the productivity of Southern agriculture.

He became widely known for his writings on farm subjects, and then used this bully pulpit to preach the doctrines of slavery, states' rights, and secession.

By 1861, Ruffin had come to hate the North with every ounce of his sixty-seven-year-old body. He admitted to having prayed on his knees that Lincoln might be elected so that it would bring on a war for Southern independence.

In December of 1860, when South Carolina held its Secession Convention, Edmund Ruffin was given the seat of honor. In the weeks that followed, he saw his picture sold all over Charleston, as the wave of Rebel patriotism began to swell toward its violent climax.

When the moment of decision finally came, Ruffin was made a temporary gun captain and led to the shore batteries that faced Fort Sumter. There he fired the cannon shot that started the Civil War. Six days later he was made an honorary member of the Palmetto Guard and even donned a Confederate uniform. Then he hobbled home to await the outcome of the struggle.

Four years later, Lee surrendered to Grant. The War was over, and no Rebel was any more disillusioned than Edmund Ruffin. So distraught was the 71 year-old that he armed himself and prepared to take aim once more. This time however, he turned the gun on himself. In one final act of defiance, the man who fired the first shot of the Civil War ended his own life rather than endure what he was sure would be the ravages of Yankee domination.

Daniel Edgar Sickles

Daniel Edgar Sickles lived most of his life in the public eye. While representing New York State in the United States Congress in 1859, he shot and killed his wife's paramour almost within the shadows of the White House. When the victim turned out to be the United States Attorney for Washington D.C., Sickles made headlines in almost every newspaper in the country.

Although the shooting was deemed "justifiable homicide," most pundits considered Sickles to have committed political suicide. But that was before his Civil War maneuvering rescued his reputation.

When the War Between the States broke out, Sickles raised a New York regiment and was made a Brigadier General. By the time of the Battle of Chancellorsville he had been promoted to Major General and given command of the Third Corps of the Army of the Potomac. That was his position on that fateful day of July 2, 1863, during the second day of fighting at the Battle of Gettysburg.

Still commanding the Third Corps, Sickles in violation

of orders, advanced on the Union Forces at the Wheat Field of Gettysburg, stretching his lines too thin and inviting an attack by the Confederates under General Longstreet. The Third Corps was plain lucky that day, but Sickles was not. A cannon ball hit his leg and it had to be amputated. Sickles' war was over.

Determined to fend off severe public criticism of his impulsive movements on July 2, Sickles ordered that his leg be preserved and sent to Washington D.C. There he accompanied it to a medical museum, thereby showing the mesmerized media the sacrifice he had made for his country. After the war, Sickles made several trips to the Washington Museum to visit his own leg, each time building considerable public sympathy. As a result, he was made Ambassador to Spain and then once more was elected to Congress. In 1895 he authored the bill creating the Gettysburg National Park.

In 1914 Daniel Sickles died and was given a hero's burial in Arlington National Cemetery. His masterful job of spin control, using his own leg, had rescued him from any serious alienation of national affection

Daniel Edgar Sickles After Amputation

Edward D. Baker

Edward D. Baker was a one-time Illinois lawyer and an intimate friend of Abraham Lincoln. He went west during the California gold rush and wound up in Oregon in 1860, where he was elected to the United States Senate.

When the Civil War broke out, no one was more pro Union than Senator Baker. "I want a sudden, bold, forward, determined war," he proclaimed after the firing on Fort Sumter. So intent was he on punishing the South that he joined the army as a Colonel while holding on to his seat in the Senate.

Colonel/Senator Edward Baker divided his time between the army and the Senate. From time to time he would return from the field, appearing in full uniform on the floor of the Senate where he would unbuckle his sword, lay it across his desktop and launch into an oratorical attack upon those of his fellow lawmakers who appeared to favor any compromise with secession.

Then on October 21, 1861, he took leave of his Senate desk to lead his regiment up Ball's Bluff, on the Potomac. His task was to cross the river and disperse the Confederate snipers who fired at will from the brush and timber atop the Bluff.

There was no doubt in Baker's mind that his troops would carry the day. He reckoned, however, without the tenacity of the Mississippi and Virginia soldiers who commanded the Bluff.

For the Rebels it was a turkey shoot. Panic quickly ran through the Union ranks, and in short order they were frantically sliding back down the Bluff and heading toward the Maryland side. As telegraphic accounts of the rout reached the President, both he and Congress awaited the fiery report from Baker that was sure to come, but this was not to be. Baker had taken to the Senate floor for his last time. His body lay back up on the Bluffs, the victim of the deadly sniper's fire that took 200 other lives.

Thus the senator who had so dramatically prodded his fellow legislators while adorned in his military garb, had fallen victim to his own rhetoric. It was one thing to harangue the halls of Congress in favor of military action. It was quite another thing to put one's own words into action. As a senator and a soldier, Edward Baker did both and paid for it with his life.

Jonathan Edwards was a great preacher, perhaps the best the 18th century had to offer. His well known sermon, "Sinners in the Hands of an Angry God," made him famous. Reverend Edwards was a straight-laced, no-nonsense Puritan, and he raised his children to be the same. It's a real pity that his grandson didn't listen.

Edwards fathered eleven children--three sons and eight daughters, one of whom, Esther, married the President of Princeton University and gave birth to a sickly son. Twice, before he was two years old, the child narrowly escaped death, so it comes as no surprise that the daughter of Jonathan Edwards determined to see that her child was brought up in a "peculiar manner" for God.

All good intentions to the contrary, however, the grandson of the man who brought America to her knees during the Great Awakening, proved to be a "dirty, little, noisy boy who was sly and mischievous." He required a strong hand to bring him to terms.

Out of a sense of obligation to his family history, the precocious lad was induced to began the study of theology, but that didn't last long. He was soon ostracized by his Church for spreading the heresy that the road to Heaven was open to just about anyone. That's when he decided to study law.

After service in the Revolutionary War, the young man opened his law practice and began to indiscriminately court the girls, most of whom he promised to marry. These activities put a strain on his pocket book, and soon he was facing a debtors' prison, so he turned to politics. By 1800, he had become the Vice-President of the United States, and he might have become the Nation's Chief Executive if he hadn't killed a former Secretary of the Treasury in a senseless duel.

He escaped a murder trial, but later became involved in yet another scandal which resulted in his being accused of treason, and by now you've guessed the identity of this child gone astray. His name was Aaron Burr, the man who shot

Alexander Hamilton and tried to incite an insurrection in Mississippi and Louisiana. Burr died in 1836, and one has to wonder what Jonathon Edwards, his Puritan grandfather would have said at the funeral of his grandson who seemed to have gone out of his way to "shake his puny fist in the face of an angry God."

Aaron Burr

President Abraham Lincoln

President Abraham Lincoln is perhaps the most revered of all American Presidents, and no small portion of this adulation has emerged from his image as the Great Emancipator. "Lincoln freed the slaves" is the household understanding of the man, but a second look at his famous Emancipation Proclamation raises a big question mark.

Lincoln issued the Emancipation Proclamation on January 1, 1863. With the stroke of a pen, the President transformed the Civil War into a struggle for human freedom. Lincoln's order freed all of the slaves within any state or part thereof that was in rebellion against the United States of America.

Thus it was that human bondage was outlawed in most

of the states of the South. Later generations extolled the virtue of this edict, but as a practical matter, it DIDN'T FREE A SINGLE SLAVE!

In the first place, the Emancipation Proclamation did nothing to eliminate the peculiar institution in Missouri, Kentucky, Maryland, or Delaware. Those slave states were loyal to the Union and unaffected by the Proclamation.

Likewise 13 parishes or counties in Louisiana and the entire state of Tennessee were exempt because by 1863, they were no longer in rebellion. West Virginia, which had seceded from Virginia was, in the words of the document, "left precisely as if this proclamation were not issued."

So it was, that in reality, Abraham Lincoln's Emancipation Proclamation freed not one single slave. In the slave states which were not in rebellion--where Lincoln could have freed the slaves--he didn't, and in those Confederate states and portions thereof which continued by force of arms to resist the Federal government--where he had no coercive power to free the slaves, he ineffectually proclaimed their freedom. In other words, the status quo prevailed.

Of course slavery was finally outlawed in the United States, but it took the 13th Amendment to the Constitution to accomplish it. The Proclamation of the Great Emancipator fell on deaf ears as long as brothers continued to kill brothers on the battlefields of the Civil War.

Throughout the course of our nation's legal history, temporary insanity has been an often used, but seldom successful, defense for murder. American juries generally have been very reluctant to accept this explanation for violent action, notwithstanding the fact that the first time it was used, it set a member of Congress free after he had taken the life of a famous American.

In February of 1859, Daniel E. Sickles, who was in Washington D.C. representing his New York constituents in Congress, was shattered by the news that his wife had been holding amorous rendezvous with his best friend in a rented apartment.

The friend, who came from a highly respected and well-known family, was the U. S. Attorney for Washington D.C. He was known to be a ladies man, but had aroused no suspicions in Sickles' mind, until he was apprised of the illicit liaison by an anonymous informant.

When Sickles confronted his wife, Theresa, with the allegation, she broke down and confessed. The equally distraught husband demanded a written confession from his wife and then sent her packing to her mother's. That left him to deal freely with Philip Barton Key, the man who had defiled his bed.

On Sunday, February 27, Sickles, while looking out across Lafayette Square from his window, spied Key walking up Pennsylvania Avenue. Enraged, he grabbed his pistol and stormed out of the house to confront his adversary.

Sickles caught up with Key almost within the shadows of the White House and put a bullet in him at point blank range. Key died there right on the street, and Congressman Sickles was arrested.

During Sickles' trial, he offered a novel defense for the time--temporary insanity. The court pondered it, and the jury bought it. Congressman Daniel E. Sickles was set free, and a celebration, which included most of the jury, was held in a nearby hotel.

Public sentiment gushed forth in support of the innocent verdict. Society would have no truck with scoundrels who trifled with the domestic relations of another man's home, not even when the defiler was the son of Francis Scott Key, author of the Star Spangled Banner. Apparently when the "Dawn's early light" revealed Philip Barton Key's dishonorable advances. The mental "rockets red glare" that ignited Sickles' passion was enough to convince a jury for the first time that temporary insanity made the killing justifiable.

Daniel Edgar Sickles

Joshua Abraham Norton

San Francisco is known throughout the United States for its tolerance of diversity. Just about any cockamamie idea or movement can find a safe haven for incubation in that City. Take for instance the case of Joshua Abraham Norton. When he declared himself "Norton the First, Emperor of the United States and Protector of Mexico, San Francisco residents nodded their assent and paid homage to His Majesty for twenty-one years.

Norton came to San Francisco in 1849, already a rich man, and his wealth continued to grow until 1859, when he lost everything in some wild rice speculation. At that point, something inside the man snapped, and he presented himself to the public as the Emperor of the United States.

Dressed in a rumpled old military uniform, Norton strode proudly into the offices of a San Francisco newspaper and gave them the notice of his self-coronation. For some reason, the editor printed it and overnight created Norton I, Emperor of the United States.

For the next two decades, Norton graced the streets of San Francisco with his presence. Citizens who passed him addressed him as "Your Majesty." Policemen saluted him smartly. He reviewed the state militia, and a special chair was always reserved for him in the state legislature. Likewise, the newspapers published a number of his imperial proclamations. In one he abolished Congress and fired both Abraham Lincoln and Jefferson Davis.

To finance his royal affairs, Norton printed his own money, which, although legally worthless, were grabbed up by tourists at above face value. To supplement his finances, Norton I, taxed all of the businesses in town and collected the 2 or 3 dollar assessments personally.

On the night of January 8, 1880, Norton I suddenly passed away. Newspapers ran the headline, "The King is Dead." Later ten thousand people filed past his casket, and his funeral cortege was two miles long. He was buried in the Masonic cemetery and on his tombstone they engraved these words, without the quotation marks, "Norton I, Emperor of the United States and Protector of Mexico, Joshua A. Norton, 1819-1880."

It seemed a fitting monument to the man who had the gumption to proclaim himself Emperor of the United States and managed to convince an entire town to humor him for more than twenty years.

The Monkey Trial of 1925

When Charles Darwin began thinking about the origin of species, he raised a ruckus that continues to this very day. At no time, however, has the debate caused more controversy than in the so-called Monkey Trial of 1925. The jury in that case returned a guilty verdict, giving a leading prosecutor a thumping victory, but he never lived to enjoy it.

It all started when a high school biology teacher by the name of John Scopes decided to test a Tennessee law which prohibited public school instructors from teaching any theory that man is descended from a lower order of animal.

Scopes was immediately indicted, and brought to trial. Overnight, the entire country focused on the town of Dayton, Tennessee. The famous defense attorney, Clarence Darrow ran to help Scopes, while William Jennings Bryan, three time Presidential candidate rushed in to advise the prosecution.

The outcome of the trial was a forgone conclusion. The judge, John Raulston, was a rural magistrate from the hamlet of

Fiery Gizzard, Tennessee, who was strongly prejudiced against the defendant. Scopes was found guilty of being in violation of the Tennessee law and fined $100.

The guilt or innocence of the teacher, however, was not what held the nation spellbound. The attraction of the trial lay in the gargantuan struggle between the liberal Darrow and the fundamentalist Bryan, who agreed to testify as an expert witness on the Bible.

The verdict of history is that the aging politician was no match for his cynical opponent. Through no efforts of his own, his side won the case, but there was a price. Bryan was publicly raked over the coals by Darrow and discredited in the minds of many. Not even the guilty verdict could raise his slumping spirits. After the trial, Bryan trudged home, and within a few days he died in his sleep, never having gained his self-confidence.

So the Scopes trial was the last battle for the aging warrior, but he did have the last word. He may not have convinced the skeptics, but the statute that set the stage for the "Monkey Trial" spectacle, although later ignored and unenforced, remained on the books. For a long time the state of Tennessee officially agreed with Bryan and denounced the theory of evolution, while at the same time turning a blind eye to his fundamentalist arguments.

In 1861, the first shots of the American Civil War were fired at Fort Sumter in Charleston Harbor. As fate would have it, the enemy commanders were well acquainted with one another, and this fact had fatal consequences for a certain private, Donald Hough.

Before the Rebels began their attack on Fort Sumter, General P.G.T. Beauregard sent a message out to Major Anderson, his old artillery instructor at West Point. The Confederate General, sure that he was going to be successful in taking the fort, informed Anderson that when the inevitable occurred, the Union commander would be given the opportunity to salute the Stars and Stripes before it was replaced with the Stars and Bars. With this understanding between the two former comrades, the ball began.

The Confederate batteries opened fire first, while Anderson and his troops remained sheltered in the covered casements, unable to do little damage to the Confederate gun positions. Finally, when it became obvious to everyone that the fort was going to fall, Anderson signaled his intention to surrender, but before he did, he was going to take advantage of his past relationship with his adversary.

So Anderson ordered his guns to make ready for the salute which Beauregard had promised. Halfway through the observance, however, one heavy gun exploded and killed Private Donald Hough instantly.

During that siege of Fort Sumter, not one soldier lost his life, but in this one act of military courtesy extended by Beauregard to Anderson as he was surrendering his position, Donald Hough was accidentally killed by "friendly fire" and became the first man to die in a war that would see the deaths of more than 600,000 other men and boys. In retrospect, it seems a pity, at least for Hough, that his commanding officer was on such friendly terms with the enemy.

Harry Love   Joaquin Murrieta

Every school child knows that Harry Love is supposed to have killed the outlaw, Joaquin Murrieta, and put his head in a jar. In the summer of 1853, newspapers all over were writing about how the California Rangers under Love had slain Murrieta. It was an ignominious end for the man whom some were calling a folk hero, but not nearly so revolting as the death of the one who received the reward for killing him.

After he collected his share of the bounty for killing Joaquin Murrieta, Harry Love settled down near Santa Cruz, California, where he married a huge, strong-willed divorcee by the name of Mary Bennett. She was tough-minded and stubborn, and after the two began to quarrel, Harry took to the bottle.

Between Mary's overbearing ways and Harry's drinking, the marriage went on the rocks. She moved to Santa Clara where she owned some property and hired a handyman by the name of Chris Everson. In a short time Chris was doing a little more than just help around the place.

On June 28, 1868, Love decided to settle the score. He rode to Mary's residence with a pistol and a shotgun and waited for her and Everson by the gate. When the couple pulled up in a buggy, Harry opened fire, and Chris did the same. A settling of the dust revealed that Everson had received some birdshot in the face and arm but was in no serious danger. Love, on the other hand, had been hit in the right arm.

A physician was called, and he decided to amputate Love's arm right there on the porch. When Harry protested, the doctor gave him a huge dose of chloroform and began to cut. Within moments the arm was off, but Harry went into shock and died.

Thus the man who allegedly cut off the head of Joaquin Murrieta was himself dismembered, and his body lies unmarked in the cemetery of Santa Clara Mission. Attempts in 1979 to erect an historical marker over his grave were abandoned because of wide-spread protests over the project. So Harry Love continues to lie unheralded in his final resting place, presumably minus an arm Such is the verdict of history on the killer of Joaquin Murrieta whose body also lies in an unmarked grave--minus his head.

Franklin Pierce

The Presidential campaign of 1852 was a rough and tumble affair, and when dark horse candidate, Franklin Pierce, captured the Democratic nomination, Mrs. Pierce was more than surprised. She was terrified. She had a strong premonition that something bad was going to happen, and it did, but it sure wasn't what she had imagined.

Two months later, in January, 1853, the train pulled away from the station in Andover, Massachusetts. It had only one passenger car, but it carried a very special traveler. Franklin Pierce, the President-elect of the United States was on his way to be sworn in as the nation's 14th Chief Executive. Mrs. Pierce and 11 year-old Benjamin sat beside him. She remained uneasy.

The train left the depot at 12:15 P.M. on that freezing January afternoon. Pierce and his family settled in to watch the countryside slip by. They would not enjoy the view for very long.

President-elect Pierce was looking out the window. It was now 12:20 P.M. Suddenly he felt a severe shock. The front axle had broken, and the car was being dragged along the tracks. In another second, it was thrown over a rocky ledge and turned over twice before it hit the bottom.

After a few moments of moans and groans, it looked as if no one had been seriously hurt and that everybody was accounted for. Then Mrs. Pierce cried out that she couldn't find Benjamin. The President-elect rushed down the embankment to the splintered car that had broken in half. There he spied his son. The father gently picked up the lifeless body and carried it back to where Mrs. Pierce was sitting. Benjamin Pierce was no longer lost.

The Pierces buried their last child and went on to Washington. The President was forced to turn from the tragedy and deal with the monumental issues that faced the country. Mrs. Pierce, however, could find no such solace. She became a recluse, unable to carry out her duties as First Lady, and she never forgave herself.

All the time, her premonitions of tragedy had caused her to fear for her husband's life. She had been afraid that someone would assassinate him. She never dreamed that the needle of her extra-sensory perception was pointing to little Benjamin, the last of her three children to be jerked from this life.

President James A. Garfield

Life looked promising for James A. Garfield in 1880. He had just been elected President of the United States after a distinguished political and military career. As fate would have it, however, his life was cut short, due in no small measure to the bed on which he was placed after he was shot by an assassin.

James Garfield was elected as the 20th President of the United States. He had been a Civil War general and a long tenured member of the House of Representatives. When he took the oath of office in March of 1881, nobody expected that just a few months later, a mournful nation would bury its second assassinated President.

On July 2, 1881, in a Washington railroad station, Charles Giteau, an embittered attorney, who had sought a consular post, shot the President. They carried the wounded Chief Executive to the White House, and there he lingered for two months.

Physicians from all over the country were called in to help save the President's life. Through all of July and August, Garfield's doctors kept their vigil, attempting to solve one very perplexing problem. The medics couldn't find the bullet in Garfield's body. They felt and probed for days on end with no luck. Finally, somebody suggested sending for Alexander Graham Bell, inventor of the telephone. Perhaps his latest invention, the metal detector, would do the job.

Alas, not even the likes of the man who invented the telephone could find that bullet. Bell's induction-balance electrical device went inexplicably haywire every time it was passed over the President's body.

On September 19, 1881, the hidden bullet did its work, and the President died from the infection it caused. It was only after his funeral, that Bell solved the mystery of the failure of his invention to find the bullet. Garfield had been placed on a bed with metal springs, and no one thought to move him.

Thus it was that in an effort to make the President comfortable, his attendants sealed his fate. Who knows? One of those old-fashioned feather beds might have changed the course of American history.

"Dr. Joe Meek"

When Americans began drifting into California in the 1840's, most of them thought that they were coming to one of the healthiest climates in the world. As a matter of fact, though, people got just as sick here as they did any place else. That's why some of the first pioneers became doctors. The only problem was none of them had any credentials.

Dr. John Marsh was the first California pioneer to become a doctor without benefit of the Hippocratic oath. He used his Harvard diploma, written in Latin, which few Californios could read, to prove that he was qualified to take care of the sick. So qualified was he, that Marsh charged 25 cow hides, the common currency of the day, for a home visit.

Marsh, the heroic fraud, was then followed by two more makeshift practitioners, Joe Meek and G.M. Waseurtz. Meek could neither read nor write, but that didn't stop him. When the colorful mountain man came down from Oregon to Monterey, he cheerfully announced that he was a physician. One of his very first patients was a young Mexican lad who had cut off his toe with an ax. Meek stuck the boy's toe back on with mud, and it grew. From then on, nobody around Monterey had any trouble referring to Meek as Doctor.

The third man to enter the medical field was Waseurtz. He too wound up in Monterey, and because of his knowledge of botany and minerals, the Natives concluded that he was a "Medico."

Waseurtz replied that since he could look grave and was looking for a business opportunity, he suddenly became a doctor. "I laid down some broad principles," wrote Waseurtz. "One was to charge well, and the other was never to prescribe anything that was not disagreeable to take."

Thus as California prepared to receive the thousands of pioneers during the gold rush, the California Medical Society consisted of Doctor John Marsh, Doctor Joe Meek, and Doctor G.M. Waseurtz, all of them charging high prices and apparently only mildly impeding the curative abilities of Mother Nature.

Light Horse Harry Lee

Robert Morris could have been a hero in American history, if he hadn't tried so hard to line his own pockets. When his fiscal bubble finally burst, he was thrown into jail, but even that wouldn't have been so bad, if only he hadn't taken a real hero down with him.

At the peak of his career, Robert Morris financed the American Revolutionary War on credit. He cornered the tobacco market, and controlled a vast empire in banking and shipping. No doubt about it, he was a brilliant tycoon, until he dreamed up that scheme for building a large town along the banks of the Potomac River.

At first blush, it looked like the perfect plan. The land could be had for a pittance, a town developed, and then lots sold at a price that would yield astronomical profits. All he needed was some additional capital, and that's why he went to Light Horse Harry Lee, the father of General Robert E. Lee.

Lee invested his family fortune in the scheme and then sat back to reap the reward--he didn't have to wait long. Come to find out, the land titles could not be cleared because of a technicality, and the whole plan went belly up. Morris and Lee both went to jail.

It was a sad spectacle, especially for Lee--the man who had been such a brilliant general in the Revolutionary War, the man who had been the Governor of Virginia, the man who as a member of Congress had stood up and eulogized George Washington as "first in war, first in peace, and first in the hearts of his countrymen"--sitting in a debtor's prison.

In 1800 Congress passed the Bankruptcy Act, which allowed Morris and Lee to be set free. The former died shortly thereafter, but Lee lived on to suffer continued humiliation at home. Finally he abandoned his family and left for the West Indies, in a solitary attempt to recover his fortunes. It was futile.

In 1818, Lee decided to return home but never made it. On the return voyage he was stricken with typhoid fever and died. He was buried by the ship's crew on Cumberland Island, Georgia. Thus Light Horse Harry Lee, with his reputation in shreds, became the final casualty in that wild speculation of Robert Morris.

Robert Morris

The Ruins of the Henry House

By all accounts, the American Civil War was the bloodiest conflict the United States has ever endured. More than 600,000 soldiers died, and this figure does not take into account the toll on the civilian population. Numerous stories of non-combatants abound, and of these, none is more poignant than that of Judith Henry.

In July of 1861, Mrs. Henry and her boys found themselves the unwilling pawns in the first real battle of the Civil War. They lived just two or three miles northwest of Manassas Junction, which was itself just 20 miles south of Washington D.C. For days the Confederate forces had been assembling around the hill upon which the Henry house sat. The family knew that it was just a matter of time until the Union army would challenge the right of a Southern army to camp so close to the nation's capital.

On July 21, 1861, the fight began, and the Henry home was caught right in the middle. With muskets popping and artillery shells exploding, Mrs. Henry's sons prepared a litter for their mother and evacuated the house. They carried her to the shelter of a nearby ravine. There they saw war at its worst.

Soon both armies were contending ferociously for control of Henry Hill, and the fighting disintegrated into hand-to-hand skirmishes. It was more than Judith Henry could take.

Amidst the smoke and groans of battle, Mrs. Henry asked that they leave the protection of the ravine and return to the house. When her sons hesitated, she insisted. She begged so piteously to be allowed to die in her own bed that they relented and brought her back, and there she had her wish. A shell hit the bedroom and killed them all the instant they laid her down. As the house began to flame, her lifeless body was riddled with bullets.

At the end of the day, silhouetted against the smoke filled horizon and flanked by torn and tattered trees were the ruins of the Henry House--all that remained of a lifetime of labor brought to an end by the horror of war.

Judith Henry was probably never counted in any wartime statistic, but she paid the ultimate price just as if she were a soldier in battle--with one huge difference. Unlike Billy Yank and Johnny Reb, she at least was able to die in her own bed.

Rutherford B. Hayes   **Samuel J. Tilden**

The election was a dead heat. The popular vote was close, and neither candidate seemed to have a majority in the electoral college. Then all eyes turned toward Florida. Does this scenario sound familiar? Actually it describes the election of 1876, when shenanigans in Florida threw the nation into a tizzy.

In that year, Republican Rutherford B. Hayes and Democrat Samuel J. Tilden were running for President. When the vote was counted in November, no one had a majority in the Electoral College. The election hinged on the 19 electoral votes in Louisiana, South Carolina, and Florida, and the results in those three states were in dispute.

Charges and counter-charges flew, and things got so ugly that Congress had to create a special commission to decide the election. Five members of the panel came from the Senate- -three Republicans and two Democrats. Five came from the House--three Democrats and two Republicans, and five came from the United States Supreme Court--two Democrats, two Republicans and one "independent" judge.

A close examination of the vote in South Carolina and Louisiana put those states in Hayes' column. Then the Commission turned to Florida. Election officials there contacted the Tilden people and offered to make it impossible for the Commission to do anything other than award the state's electoral votes to him, and the price for such an assurance?--$200,000 dollars.

"That seems to be the standard figure," Tilden remarked to a friend before he rejected the offer. The Democratic candidate was sure he wouldn't need it. He was certain that under the scrutiny of the Federal Election Commission, he would be awarded Florida's electors.

Much to Tilden's surprise, however, the Commission gave Florida--and the election--to Rutherford B. Hayes, who became the nation's 18th President. Tilden had prevailed in the popular vote by a margin of 247,000 votes, but in the Electoral College the tally stood at 185 to 184 in favor of Hayes and all because Tilden refused a bribe. One has to wonder how much things have changed in the Sunshine State over the past century or so?

Adolf Hitler

Nearly every school child has seen those famous photographs of the Hindenburg, the most majestic of all of the German airships, reduced to flames in 1937. In the aftermath of the disaster, a multiplicity of causes were given, but few put the blame where it should have been placed--squarely on the shoulders of Adolf Hitler.

It was 7:25 on the morning of May 6, 1937, and the Hindenburg was attempting a landing at Lakehurst, New Jersey, after making its 20th transoceanic flight. As it dropped its mooring lines to the ground crew 200 feet below, the giant craft burst into flames. Twenty-seven passengers jumped to their deaths rather than face the terrifying fire.

After the official body count, 36 people were found to have lost their lives in the destruction of the Hindenburg, including one American member of the ground crew.

Following this unprecedented disaster, most of the experts blamed an atmospheric electrical spark that supposedly ignited the gas that was flowing from a leak in the ship. The fact that the outer cover of the tail section was fluttering just seconds before the explosion gave support to this theory. Still others pointed to the high volatility paint used on the airship, which would have been something akin to coating it in rocket fuel.

All of these scientific explanations, however, fail to take note of the political climate of the time, and herein we may find the ultimate cause of the burning of the Hindenburg. The huge blimp had been designed to be lifted by helium. This gas, however, was scarce at the time, and the United States refused to sell any to Germany, which had just been taken over by the extremist, Adolf Hitler. The American Government suspected that the Germans might soon have military plans for their airships. Thus, the Hindenburg was forced to turn to the highly flammable gas, Hydrogen, seven million cubic feet of it, instead of helium. One has to wonder if the Nazi dictator, whose bellicose rantings and ravings spread fear throughout the world, wasn't at least indirectly responsible for the destruction of his own airship.

William P. Huff

In early 1849 news of the discovery of gold in California spread across the country like wildfire. In the words of Texan William P. Huff, "The heated brains of many, through a delusive but sudden hope, built fortunes as well as castles in the air with that gold which lay in the sands or locked up in the Quartz bound hills and mountains of the distant land of Ophir."

By April 22, 1849, Huff had been smitten sufficiently with gold fever to bid his family good-bye. He gathered his wife Mary, who was 7 months pregnant, and his children and placed them in the care of an old friend. Then he set out across the rugged frontier to the mines of Mariposa, certain that he would strike it rich.

Huff panned in the streams of Agua Fria Creek, Bear Creek, and Mariposa Creek without success. By late 1852, he returned home penniless and heartbroken to find that while he was gone, his wife had died in childbirth.

William P. Huff never recovered from the debilitating effects of his gold fever. He lost his drive--his spirit--his nerve, and by the time they laid him to rest in Houston in 1886, he was on the dole.

Later, local historians further tarnished Huff's memory by labeling him impractical, impecunious, and a ne'er-do-well. Then in 1986, one hundred years after his death, Huff's fortunes revived.

Mrs. David Ewing Stewart, wife of Huff's great-great grandson made a startling discovery. While cleaning out an old cedar chest that had been handed down in her husband's family, she found two old, tattered, leather-bound ledger books.

Mrs. Stewart's first impulse was to throw them away with all of the other trash. Then she opened the covers, and to her surprise she found that they contained a daily account of William P. Huff's journey to California in 1849!

Curious as to the value of Huff's journal, the Stewart's sought out appraiser John Payne who, not too long before, had established the value of the Nixon papers. After studying the documents, Payne called the Stewarts with the good news. What they had was the most comprehensive diary coming out of the southern trails in 1849. Payne set the value of Huff's work at $300,000!

That old Texan may have been impecunious and impractical. He might even have been a ne'er-do-well, but this one thing is certain. He sure didn't return to California empty handed. He knew the value of history.

Mr. and Mrs. James F. Reed

James F. Reed was a very prosperous Illinois merchant. He lived not far from Abraham and Mary Lincoln on 8th Street in Springfield. In 1846, Reed decided to join the Donner party in their tragic trek west, but before they got to California, Reed was banished from the group and was left in the desert to die. As things turned out, however, that punishment wound up saving his life.

After reaching Fort Bridger, the ill-fated Donner Party made the mistake of taking the Hastings Cut-off and lost 30 to 40 days in so doing. Nerves became frayed and tempers ran short. Two of Reed's companions, John Synder and Milt Elliot began to quarrel, and when Reed intervened, Synder beat him with a bull whip. James defended himself with a knife and sank it deep into Snyder's chest.

On October 5, 1846, the party held a meeting and decreed that although his family could remain, James Frazier

Reed would have to go. He was banished without gun or food into the wilderness. Meanwhile, the rest of the Donner Party plodded on toward their rendezvous with destiny.

By November 1, 1846, the group was just 3 miles from the summit of the Sierra Nevada when the first hard snows hit. They were trapped. Several aborted attempts were made to breach the pass, but they failed, and as everyone knows the Donner Party had to resort to cannibalism.

Then in February of 1847, who should appear in their camp but James F. Reed. He had made it to Sutter's Fort all by himself and now led a rescue party back to his family and stranded comrades--the very ones who had consigned him to death in the desert just a few months prior.

In the end, 45 members of the Donner Party survived while 34 perished, and among those who made it were the Reeds. While their father's expulsion had all the trappings of a tragedy at the time, it was in reality a blessing in disguise. Who knows what would have happened to the family if they had been forced to stay up in those mountains where human flesh was all that kept some people alive.

Jefferson Davis

General Zachary Taylor was a proud man, and he wanted the very best for his family, especially his daughter, Knox Taylor. From her father's vantage point, no one was good enough for the young woman, not even the young lieutenant who sought her hand. "Young Love," however, prevailed and it cost the young bride her life.

In 1835, when a romance developed between his young subordinate and his daughter, Old Rough and Ready put his foot down. There was no way he would give his blessing to the match. He knew the strain that Army life put on a marriage.

At first the Lieutenant's southern pride was ruffled, and he contemplated challenging Taylor to a duel. Instead, he resigned his commission and married the 16 year-old girl anyway. Seeking refuge from the wrath of his father-in-law, the groom then took his bride to Hurricane, his plantation home on the Mississippi River.

Living life as the wife of a Southern aristocrat at first agreed with Knox Taylor. She managed the "big house," while her husband saw to the details of his first cotton crop. Everything was coming up roses, and then suddenly both husband and wife came down with swamp fever. Within three months, she was dead.

The grief stricken husband went into seclusion for more than a decade, but when the Mexican/American War broke out, he took command of a volunteer regiment, the Mississippi Rifles, and who do you think was his commanding General? Yes, you guessed it, his former father-in law, Zachary Taylor.

The two men gave each other a wide berth, until the Battle of Buena Vista, when troops led by the young officer defeated the Mexican Cavalry and saved the day for Taylor. After the dust settled, General Taylor sought out the hero of the battle. The two men eyed each other, and Taylor, offered these words to the younger man: "Sir, my daughter was a better judge of men than I was." With that they parted and continued to travel down different roads. General Taylor became President of the United States, while his former son-in-law, the man who stole his daughter away, Jefferson Davis, became President of the Confederate States of America. One has to wonder how history might have been changed if only 16 year-old Knox Taylor Davis had survived.

Madera County Courthouse

America's courtrooms are generally calm and deliberative places. Justice is rendered with decorum, but it wasn't always that way. Back in the olden days nobody was safe from a punch in the nose, as one case in Madera, California shows.

The whole affair started out peacefully enough but soon turned into a bonafide courtroom brawl. The two lawyers actually attacked each other right in the Madera County Courthouse and right under the nose of Superior Court Judge William Conley. When the fist stopped flying, most folks figured that would be the end of it, but little did they know just how mad those barristers were.

The opponents in the 1902 fray were H. H. Welsh, an attorney from Fresno, and W. H. Larew, a well-known Madera lawyer. Welsh, taking umbrage at Larew's intimation that he was a liar, walked over to his adversary and landed a haymaker on his cheek. After recovering from the blow, Larew danced around the courtroom, jabbing at Welsh's head. Finally the two lawyers were separated, and Judge Conley called them both to the bench to inquire why they should not be cited for contempt of court.

Conley, feeling lenient, let the attorneys off with a lecture and sent them to lunch, thinking that the matter was settled. How wrong he was! As the two men left the courthouse, they were seen in animated conversation. Then a curious thing happened. Larew shook his head in the affirmative and pointed east up Yosemite Avenue. Welsh nodded, and they began to walk together, followed by a crowd of delighted Maderans. The entourage crossed the railroad tracks and when they reached the Madera Athletic Hall, they went inside. Now it was obvious to everyone. Satisfaction was going to be had by somebody in a boxing ring.

It didn't take long to settle the matter. In less than twenty minutes, the two men left the Hall to return to court, and it was obvious that they had put on the gloves. Larew had a black eye and a goose egg on his forehead. By the same token, Welsh didn't have a mark on him. The lawyers went back to work and not a hint of hostility surfaced throughout the remainder of the trial. The dignity of Judge Conley's court had been restored without His Honor even having to raise his voice.

General Stonewall Jackson

It's no secret that General Stonewall Jackson had some strange ideas about health matters. Some historians have even called this great Civil War General a hypochondriac and insist that, had it not been for his unusual beliefs, he might not have died from that wound he received at the Battle of Chancellorsville.

Although he was one of the most talented field commanders in American history, Jackson thought of himself as "out of balance," and even under fire in battle, he was given to raising one arm in order that the blood would flow down his body and establish equilibrium.

As for his diet, he refused to eat pepper on the grounds that it made his left leg weak. He often sucked on lemons, believing that they cured his "dyspepsia," and his staff knew that even on the march, he would want his raspberries, bread, and milk for medicinal purposes.

The General was comfortable only when in a bolt upright position, with his organs held "naturally," one atop another. That's why he spent hours standing up while reading the Bible.

Jackson's list of physical complaints was as long as his arm. He imagined that he suffered from rheumatism, chilblains, neuralgia, biliousness, and a distortion of the spine. None of this, however, would have made any difference if only he hadn't insisted upon treating his own ailments.

To rid himself of nearsightedness, Jackson often dipped his head into a basin of cold water, eyes wide open, for as long as he could hold his breath. On other occasions he attempted to relieve all types of pain by applying ice cold towels to his body, and it was this last procedure that cost him his life.

After he was wounded by his own men at Chancellorsville, surgeons had to amputate one of his arms, and while he was recovering, one of his servants applied the General's usual remedy for pain. Without the knowledge of attending physicians, they placed the cold towels on Jackson's body. Within hours he contracted pleurisy and pneumonia and died.

So the South lost one of its greatest generals, and Robert E. Lee lost his right hand man. The eccentricities of the old soldier which had won him such acclaim on the battlefield finally turned against him, proving once again that "he who doctors himself has a fool for a patient."

President Andrew Jackson

President Andrew Jackson was a bare-knuckled brawler in more ways than one. He always stood his ground against his opponents, whether it was on the streets of Nashville or on Capitol Hill. He was not above rolling in the mud in a street fight, leveling a pistol in a duel, or impaling his enemies on the point of a political spear.

It is not surprising then to learn that Jackson was the first American President to become the target of an assassination. The attack occurred on January 30, 1835. Jackson was on Capitol Hill to attend the funeral services for Congressman Warren R. Davis. As the President filed past the casket and descended to the rotunda, Richard Lawrence, an unemployed house painter, stepped up, drew a pistol, and fired point blank at the former General.

A percussion cap exploded, but a bullet failed to discharge from the gun barrel. Characteristically, Jackson charged his would-be killer with complete abandon and contempt, while his breathless Vice-President, Martin Van Buren looked on, horrified.

Lifting his cane above his head, the 67 year-old Jackson lunged at his assailant. Before he could reach him, however, Lawrence drew a second pistol and fired again. Unbelievably, this gun also failed to fire.

After the second attempt failed and some semblance of order was restored, Jackson went about his business as if nothing had ever happened. As for Lawrence, he spent the rest of his life in Washington's Government Hospital for the Insane.

And Vice-President Van Buren? He gave the near tragedy considerable thought. Folks didn't call him the "Red Fox" for nothing. From that day on, Martin Van Buren never came to Capitol Hill unprepared. As the President of the Senate, he was obligated to preside over the proceedings of that body, but he didn't have to expose himself to unnecessary risks. For the remainder of his term as Vice President, Van Buren never took his place on the floor of the Senate without two pistols on his person.

Andrew Jackson may have been the first U.S. President to draw an assassin's aim, but Martin Van Buren had the distinction of becoming the first pistol-packing presiding officer of the United States Senate.

Chief Justice John Marshall

The United States has endured many Constitutional crises, but none with the poignancy of the hanging of old Corn Tassel. When this Cherokee Indian was put to death for the murder of a fellow tribesman in 1830, it set President Andrew Jackson against the United States Supreme Court and for a time put the Constitutional system of checks and balances in danger.

Corn Tassel was a member of the Cherokee tribe, located in northwestern Georgia. His people had created a state within a state, complete with a written constitution. While the United States recognized the Cherokee Nation, the state of Georgia did not. It passed a law in 1828, declaring that all Cherokee statutes were null and void.

Therefore, when in 1830, Corn Tassel, in a fit of rage, shot one of his neighbors, Georgia authorities arrested him over the objections of the Tribal Council and prepared to put him on trial.

Corn Tassel appealed to the United States Supreme Court on the basis that the crime for which he was arrested took place, not in Georgia, but within the accepted boundaries of the Cherokee Nation.

Chief Justice John Marshall, having already ruled that the Cherokee Nation was a viable political entity, declared that the action of the sheriff in Georgia was unconstitutional. He ordered Corn Tassel to be returned to the Cherokee elders.

At that point, President Andrew Jackson intervened in the dispute by assuming jurisdiction. He had wanted for a long time to move all of the Indians west of the Mississippi River and into the Indian Territory, a place which would one day become Oklahoma.

Jackson sent federal marshals to Georgia to enforce his policy, and when reminded that the United States Supreme Court had ruled contrary to that position, the President responded, "Well, Chief Justice Marshall has made his decision. Now let him enforce it."

That, of course, did it for poor old Corn Tassel and his tribe. Georgia hanged him and destroyed the independence of the Cherokee Nation, while the Supreme Court looked on helplessly. For the first time in the Constitutional history of the Republic, the Executive Branch went nose to nose with the Judiciary, and the Judge blinked.

Thomas Jefferson and John Adams

Thomas Jefferson and John Adams may have been political enemies, but their lives were really not all that different.. They were co-authors of the Declaration of Independence. They both were elected President of the United States, and with more than a touch of irony, the two men faced the Grim Reaper in an amazing coincidence.

When the people of the United States chose George Washington in the nation's first presidential election in 1789, they also installed John Adams as Vice-President. Washington then appointed Thomas Jefferson as his first Secretary of State, setting the stage for a political fight that would carry on for a decade or more.

Although Jefferson and Adams had stood side by side against King George III, after independence was won, they had drifted apart politically. Jefferson was much more democratic while Adams kept his aristocratic New England bearings. Such was the cleavage between them that when Washington declined a third term in 1796, Jefferson ran against Adams and lost.

By 1800, Adams was all set for a second term, but Jefferson campaigned hard against him. He charged that while Adams sided with the rich folks, he, Jefferson, stood for the common man. It was an effective argument, given Adams' natural propensity towards aloofness, and when the votes were finally counted, Jefferson won.

Adams went back home to nurse his political wounds in Massachusetts, while Jefferson went to the nation's new capital, Washington D. C. He served two terms and then retired to his beloved Monticello in Virginia.

Over the years, the two old patriots laid down their political swords, and grew friendly. Then the 93 year-old Adams became ill in the summer of 1826 and died. Before he breathed his last, however, he whispered the words, "Thank God, Thomas Jefferson still survives," but he was wrong. Thomas Jefferson joined John Adams in death that very day, July 4th, 1826, but three hours earlier--exactly 50 years after they both had signed the Declaration of Independence.

The Lincoln Funeral Train

When President Lincoln was assassinated in 1865, Mary Lincoln decided to bury him in their hometown of Springfield, Illinois. His body was prepared, citizens of Washington DC. said their good-byes, and the funeral train pulled out of the station.

Lincoln's family was understandably grief-stricken, but oddly enough, only one of them made that long train trip with him back to Illinois. His wife, Mary Todd Lincoln was so overwrought, she couldn't be seen in public and needed young Tad Lincoln to remain with her. Robert Todd Lincoln was able to go only as far as Baltimore. That left just little Willie to accompany his father on that long journey home.

Willie had been born in Springfield in 1850. Of all of the Lincoln children, he was most like his father. He took an early interest in politics and religion and was a keen observer of everything around him.

In Illinois, he had been his father's constant companion, even when the elder Lincoln traveled to Chicago on business. Where the father went, the son was sure to follow. That was as true as much in death as it was in life.

It took 13 days to bring Lincoln's body back to Springfield, and Willie rode with him every mile of the way. North to New York City--West to Chicago--South to Springfield, and at scores of stops in between, mourners paid homage to the fallen President, and Willie was right there.

When they took President Lincoln to Oak Ridge Cemetery in Springfield, Willie went right with him. He and his father would remain inseparable right to the end. Not even the tomb could keep them apart, for you see, young Willie Lincoln, like his father, had passed from this life as well.

In the winter of 1862, he had contracted typhoid fever and on February 20 of that year he died. Willie was buried in Georgetown, but when the President began his last trip home, they exhumed Willie and put him on the train with his father. The two caskets were carried across the country side by side, and when it came time for burial, they laid Willie to rest right beside his father. For 11 years they had been inseparable, and now not even the grave could divide them. Now they both belonged to the ages--together.

President Abraham Lincoln

Abraham Lincoln was a man full of apparent contradictions. He could be as serious as death one moment and telling funny stories the next. Today he might conduct himself as a statesman, and tomorrow he might exhibit the manners of a hillbilly. This incongruence extended right up to his last conscious moment, with the last words that he would ever hear.

The date was April 14, 1865. The place was Ford's Theater in Washington D.C. For four long years, the President had labored under the stress of leading the nation in a bloody Civil War. Now it was all over. The Union had been preserved, and he could at last relax.

As the Lincolns took their seats in the Presidential box that Friday evening, their conversation centered around a desired trip to the Holy Land, which sentiment was entirely out of keeping with the play on stage, a story about an American backwoodsman who was visiting his refined English cousins.

Harry Hawk, the company stage manager who was doubling as the male comic lead, was raucously reciting the last words that the President would ever hear. On stage, a scheming mother had just discovered the American Cousin to be poor and mannerless.

"So I don't know the manners of good society, eh?' Hawk intoned." As he recited his lines, John Wilkes Booth, having gained entrance to the box, raised his pistol. "Well, I guess I know enough to turn you inside out, old gal," spouted Hawk on stage. Booth put the gun to the back of the President's head.

"You sockdolgizing old mantrap," mouthed Hawk, These were the last words that Abraham Lincoln ever heard. Booth pulled the trigger at that very instant.

Thus the man who so eloquently framed the nation's sentiment in his Gettysburg Address; the man whose intellect sparkled in the felicity of his language; the man who believed that words were more powerful than the sword, died with the words of a pun-filled comedy filling his ears.

President Abraham Lincoln

After a week of rain, the morning of April 14, 1865, was beautiful and bright. The war was over. It had lasted so long--this war between America and itself. More than 600,000 men had perished--Union and Confederate. Now no more boys would have to die--no more wasted blood.

On this the last morning of Abraham Lincoln's life, no one could miss noticing the difference about him. He just felt good again--all except for those dreams he kept having.

The President had planned an evening at Ford's theatre

for later that night. He had invited General and Mrs. Grant, but they declined. Curiously, thirteen other people proceeded to turn Lincoln down. In the end, however, Major Rathbone and his fiancee, Clara Harris, agreed to accompany Mr. and Mrs. Lincoln.

At an 11:00 meeting of the cabinet that day, the President remarked that he had had two dreams that seemed so real. One related to water. Lincoln said he seemed to be in some vessel moving very fast. "I'm in a boat, and I drift and I drift. Gentlemen, something extraordinary is going to happen and very soon. "The cabinet members twisted uncomfortably in their chairs, and then the President told them about the other dream he had a week earlier.

He had been stirred from his slumbers in a cold sweat. It had seemed so real and had been haunting him ever since. "I heard subdued sobs," reported the President, as if a number of people were weeping. I left my bed and wandered downstairs. I went from room to room until I arrived at the East Room, which I entered. There before me was a corpse wrapped in funeral vestments. Around it were stationed soldiers who acted as guards. "Who is dead in the White House?" I demanded of one of the soldiers. "The President," was his answer. He was killed by an assassin.

Every one knows the rest of the story. Lincoln was shot that night and died the next morning. It is all part of history. What we can't explain are his dreams. Did the President have a premonition of his death? That we will most likely never know, but Lincoln said at the time, "Most people nowadays regard dreams as foolish."

Still, it is interesting to ponder how history might have been changed if only the President had given his dreams a little more credence.

Lincoln's Funeral Procession

After Abraham Lincoln's assassination , a mortified nation felt obligated to do for him in death what it had been unable to do in life--that was to give him the full dignity that he deserved. They carried his remains to a tomb and declared that "Now he belonged to the ages." Unfortunately it would be another 36 years before his body would rest in peace.

On May 4, 1865, Abraham Lincoln's remains were placed in a limestone vault in Springfield's Oak Ridge Cemetery. In less than a year, they were removed to a temporary vault higher up the hill. Then in 1871, the almost completed Lincoln Tomb at the top of the hill received the body of the President, but he still was not to rest in peace.

In the autumn of 1876, a group of counterfeiters hatched a plan whereby they would break into the tomb, steal the body, and hold it for ransom. It almost worked. Lincoln's coffin was half out the door when lawmen swooped down and put an end to the caper.

Fearful of another attempt, Lincoln's friends now hid his coffin in a labyrinth of passageways beneath the obelisk at the top of the hill, and for the next ten years, the public paid homage to an empty sarcophagus. Finally in 1901, Robert Todd Lincoln decided that enough was enough.

He ordered a hole, thirteen feet deep, to be dug below the main catacomb floor. A four-foot base of cement was laid and an iron cage sunk into it. Then Lincoln's coffin was brought to the new burial site, but before he was lowered into his new resting place, an enterprising plumber cut a little window in the coffin, just above Lincoln's face--just to make sure it was really him. To the 17 people who peeked in, there was no question. The mole was there. He still had his beard, nose, and chin--no doubt about it, it was Lincoln.

Today the body of Abraham Lincoln lies encased in tons of concrete, finally safe from all tampering or any other disturbance, short of a strong earthquake, and no longer susceptible to the prying eyes of the curious. Now he really does belong only to the Ages.

Lincoln's Replica Coffin

President Abraham Lincoln

The assassination of Abraham Lincoln by John Wilkes Booth has fascinated historians for years. Books, papers, and treatises on the tragedy abound, but a lot more could be written if scholars would take seriously the strange events that followed the death of our 16th President.

Consider Henry and Clara Rathbone, the young couple who attended Ford's theatre with the Lincolns. They later moved to Germany, and he lost his mind, killed his wife, and ended up in an insane asylum.

Boston Corbett, the soldier who shot John Wilkes Booth, went berserk during an 1887 meeting of the Kansas State Legislature. He was arrested and sent to the Topeka Asylum for the Insane.

William A Petersen, the German tailor in whose house the President died, committed suicide in 1871.

Ann Surratt, who tried to see President Andrew Johnson to plead for clemency for her mother, who was about to be executed for conspiring to kill the President, was prevented from doing so by two men: ex-Senator Preston King, and Senator James H. Lane.

On November 13, 1865, King tied a bag of bullets around his neck and committed suicide by jumping off a ferry boat on the Hudson River. The next year, on July 11, Lane shot himself to death in Fort Leavenworth, Kansas.

During the weeks following the assassination, Mary Todd Lincoln received a great deal of comfort in the White House from Dr. Anson G. Henry, who accompanied her back to Illinois. A few months later, on July 30, 1865, Dr. Henry drowned when the steamer in which he was a passenger, sank off the coast of California.

And as for Mary Todd Lincoln herself, a jury found her "... a fit person to be in a state hospital for the insane," and that's where she wound up in 1875.

Nearly everyone who was even remotely connected to the assassination of Lincoln suffered some devastating personal tragedy. If we didn't know better, we might think that a curse of some sort had been placed on those surrounding President Lincoln, including his own family.

Abraham and Tad Lincoln

Legacies are such interesting things. One solitary life often reverberates through the ages to influence generation upon generation. The descendants of John D. Rockefeller, Henry Ford, and Joseph Kennedy provide abundant examples. One that doesn't fit the mold, however, is Abraham Lincoln, and there's a very good reason for that.

At first blush, one would expect that being a direct descendant of Abraham Lincoln today would carry with it the aura and responsibility of Noblesse Oblige, but a close look at Lincoln's descendants reveals that nothing could be further from the truth.

Abraham Lincoln and Mary Todd Lincoln had four children, all boys: Robert, Edward, Willie, and Tad. Of these offspring, only Robert lived to maturity and provided the Lincolns with grandchildren. Edward died first, before Abraham was elected President. Willie went next in 1862, while the Lincolns were in the White House, and Tad lived just a few years after his father's tragic death. By 1871, just one of the offspring of Abraham Lincoln, Robert Todd Lincoln, survived.

Robert ultimately married, and he and his wife became the parents of three children, two daughters and a son. The boy, who was named Abraham after his grandfather, died at the age of 17, while his father was minister to Great Britain. That left the two daughters to vouchsafe the legacy of Abraham Lincoln.

In time each of the granddaughters of Abraham Lincoln married, one to a Mr. Isham and the other to a Mr. Beckwith. They each in turn gave birth to a single child, both boys. The Isham lad died early and without issue. At that point all hopes for keeping the Lincoln legacy in the family rested upon Robert Todd Lincoln Beckwith, the great-grandson of Abraham Lincoln.

Then in 1986, Beckwith died in his Washington D.C. home at the age of 86 and without heirs. Thus it was in that year, Abraham Lincoln's line came to an abrupt end. Today our 16th President has no direct descendants. Now only a grateful nation is left to carry his legacy. Come to think of it, that might not be so bad after all.

Robert Todd Lincoln

Robert Todd Lincoln lived a life filled with irony. As a young lad, he was rescued from a moving train by Edwin Booth, the elder brother of John Wilkes Booth, his father's assassin, but this was just the beginning of the strange twists of fate that Robert would encounter throughout his life.

Upon graduating from Harvard University, Lincoln joined the army and was assigned to General Ulysses S. Grant's staff. Later he served the United States as the last Minister to Great Britain, before the title was changed to Ambassador, and as United States Secretary of War under Garfield. He later became President of the Pullman Company of Chicago. Thus it was that on three occasions history was able to place Robert at the scene of a national tragedy.

He was in Washington D.C. on April 14, 1865, the night that his father was shot, and upon hearing the news rushed to his bedside where he maintained a vigil until the stricken President passed away. This, however, was not the last time that he would see a President die.

In 1881, Robert Todd Lincoln, as Secretary of War, was traveling with President James A. Garfield when he was shot in the Washington D.C. railroad station, and was with him when he later died.

Then in 1901, who do you think was invited to attend the Pan-American Exposition in Buffalo New York with President William McKinley? Robert Todd Lincoln! Thus he was on hand to witness the shooting of the 25th President of the United States and the third to be assassinated.

After the death of McKinley, Robert Todd Lincoln refused to attend any future presidential functions, and retired to his summer retreat in Manchester Vermont, where he became a virtual recluse in his later years.

In 1926, Robert Todd Lincoln died, and they buried him in Vermont. Thus he became the only member of his father's immediate family not to be buried in the Lincoln family plot in Springfield, Illinois--one final twist to a life filled with strange coincidences.

Vicksburg, Mississippi

Historical truth can be an elusive thing, especially when it comes to some of those Civil War stories. One such case is that of the minie-ball pregnancy, and we want to advise our readers right here at the start that their credulity is going to be stretched just a bit before this one is over.

In the November 7, 1874, issue of the American Medical Weekly is an article written by a Dr. L. G. Capers Jr. entitled "Notes from the Diary of a Field and Hospital Surgeon, C.S.A."

According to Dr. Capers, On May 12, 1863, he beheld a young comrade fall suddenly to the ground. The medic ran to offer aid and found a compound fracture of the left tibia caused by a minie-ball which had then ricocheted from there upward through the man's body and out his groin.

As the Dr. dressed the wounds of the poor fellow, a woman came running from the porch of a nearby house. One of her daughters also had been wounded. Hastening to treat the young lady, Capers found that she too had received a minie-ball wound. It had penetrated the left abdominal region. Dr. Capers did what he could, but then had to retreat. After the battle, Capers was able to visit the young woman frequently, and just 278 days from the date of the receipt of the wound by the minie-ball, he "delivered this same young lady of a fine boy, weighing 8 pounds."

About three weeks after the birth, Dr. Capers was called to examine the baby and extracted a mashed and battered minie-ball from the child.

At that point, the doctor claims to have solved a mystery. He wrote, "The ball I took from the babe was the identical one which, on the 12th of May, shattered the tibia of the young soldier, and in its mutilated condition, plunged through his groin, and into the left ovary and the uterus of the girl, impregnating her!"

Now as for the truth of this story, your guess is as good as ours. However, as they point out in a Vicksburg, Mississippi museum, if it is true, we suppose that makes the little baby the world's one and only, honest to goodness "son-of-a-gun."

The woman loved to play the piano. She had been raised on classical music and was one of Fresno's most civilized residents in an era when refinement was rare. Often her only audience was her two year old son, but that made little difference. She was a cultural oasis in a desert of crudeness. One day however, her playing caused a great deal of alarm while giving portents of the future.

The young mother knew that her infant son was sensitive to sound. Cats fighting would make him scream and cry, and any sound of distress would draw tears. She never dreamed, however, that her piano playing would have the same effect.

One summer afternoon in 1877, while her child was occupying himself with his toys, she decided to practice a new piece. It started out as a very lively tune, but then changed to a weird, sad minor key. When the music shifted, the boy screamed out and cried so bitterly that the mother was frightened. Through his sobs, she heard him say, "Music cry, Mommy, Music cry. The woman immediately played a merry little refrain, whereupon the little one regained his composure.

Thinking that she might have been mistaken as to the cause of his tears, later in the day she played the same song again, and once more the child dropped everything and came running. With lips quivering and tears flowing, he screamed, "Stop, Mama, Stop; Music cry." There could be no doubt; her son was different; he was born with a true artistic temperament and the full range of feelings that such people have.

Before he was five, the child was cutting and drawing, and by the time he was a teenager he had taken up painting. In 1892, he left Fresno for San Francisco, and there he made it big. For you see, that two year old baby who cried at his mother's sad music--that five year old child who learned to draw on the living room floor in the house on Van Ness Street--that 12 year old lad who took up painting in the 1880's was none other than Maynard Dixon, the famous artist of the West.

Maynard Dixon

Captain Russel Perry Mace

Every town has its heroes--its pioneers--those folks who paved the way for everyone to follow. They appear almost out of nowhere to play their parts in laying the foundations for future generations. Captain Russel Perry Mace was one such individual. He was larger than life. That's why it's puzzling to ponder the way he has been ignored in death.

Captain Mace represented his county for three terms in the California State Assembly, and such was his influence among his colleagues that upon his departure from the legislature they presented him with a huge rocking chair.

In 1872, Mace opened up a hotel in the little railroad town of Borden, and when he heard that the California Lumber Company was going to lay out the village of Madera, he purchased the first lot in the town site and built its first building--Mace's Yosemite Hotel.

Thus Captain Russel Perry Mace became Madera's first citizen. His hotel became a showplace for the valley, and such luminaries as Ulysses S. Grant, Rutherford B. Hayes, and John C. Fremont were his guests at one time or another.

For the next couple of decades, Captain Mace was Madera's leading citizen and chief promoter. The town had no more enthusiastic booster. He could be seen every day, wearing his ubiquitous top hat and carrying his gold handled cane, greeting folks along the wooden sidewalks of his home town. He was the nearest thing that Madera had to a mayor in those days before incorporation.

Then in 1894, his eating habits caught up with him. His morbid obesity took his life, and he was buried in Madera's Arbor Vitae Cemetery amidst widespread mourning. Such was the esteem with which he was held that the railroad ran special trains to Madera from Fresno for his funeral.

Today, one can visit Captain Mace in Arbor Vitae Cemetery, but one has to look closely for his grave, for you see, this old pioneer--Madera's first citizen has no tombstone! For 110 years he has had only a crude cement slab to mark his final resting place. It seems rather curious that such a grave injustice would be allowed. Perhaps it's time to fix it.

Minnie Marx

Minnie was known as the woman who taught her children to be fools, and that's probably the truth, but there's much more to the story than that. While she trained her sons in the art of slapstick comedy, she also embedded in them the eternal principle of all performers, "the show must go on," no matter what.

Without the guiding hand of Minnie Marx, the world would probably have been deprived of the wonderful, zany, humor of the Marx brothers. She was their agent, their manager, their severest critic, and their most appreciative audience. She was also the force that drove them on.

It was Minnie who cajoled a neighbor to teach Chico Marx to play the piano. It was Minnie who got Groucho his first job in Gus Edwards' vaudeville act, and it was Minnie who screamed and argued for all of her sons until they finally found their niche in the entertainment world.

She lived to see an achievement greater even than her

wildest hopes--the popularizing of the Marx Brothers. She went to see their first motion picture 51 times! Then came that fateful evening when her boys were playing "Animal Crackers" in New York. Mama and Papa Marx had had an early dinner and were preparing to go to the theater. Suddenly Minnie seized her husband's arm. "Give me the mirror, Sam," she said. "I think I got a stroke." She never spoke again.

A doctor was called, and the boys were advised by telephone of what had happened. Harpo, Groucho, Chico, and Zeppo didn't even have to think. They immediately set about doing the only thing their mother would have allowed them to do.

They went through the ultimate ordeal of actors--to laugh, to jest, to carry on the show--while their mother lay dying. When the final curtain had been rung down, the four clowns, still in make-up, hurried to reach their mother before it was too late.

Their father met them at the foot of the stairs and took them to her room. They stared at the lifeless form on the bed and wept over the body of Minnie Marx. They had not been in time to tell her good-bye, but they had preserved a family tradition. Never disappoint the audience. Keep the people laughing. Minnie would have been very, very proud of her boys.

Pioneer Wagon Train

One of the strangest tales in American history is recorded in the diary of Elizabeth Geer. She and her husband and their seven children set out in a covered wagon from Indiana headed for California in 1847. The wagon train with which the Geers were traveling reached the half way point by September 15. On the morning of the 16th, one of the men reported that he was having trouble.

His wife was angry at him for trying to drag her half way across the continent and refused to take another step west. Not only would she not budge, she wouldn't allow her children to go either. Her husband had had his oxen hitched up to the wagons for three hours and had been coaxing her to hop aboard, but she wouldn't stir.

Elizabeth told her husband what was taking place, and he gathered three male companions and went to consult with the recalcitrant woman. When she steadfastly refused their entreaties to join them, they grabbed her young ones and crammed them in the wagon. Her husband then drove off and left her sitting.

As the wagons rolled west, the abandoned woman got up, took the back track and traveled out of sight. Meanwhile, the husband sent his oldest son back to where they had camped to retrieve a horse that he had left. In less than an hour, having cut across a bend in the road, the wife overtook her husband. When he saw her he asked, "Did you meet Son John?"

"Yes" was the reply, "and I picked up a stone and knocked out his brains."

Her stunned husband went back to ascertain the truth, and while he was gone, she set his wagon, which was loaded with all of their store bought goods, on fire, The cover was completely burned, as were some valuable articles. When the man saw the flames, he came running back to put them out. According to Elizabeth, when this was accomplished, "The husband finally mustered spunk enough to give his wife what she needed: a good flogging."

Unfortunately, Mrs. Geer doesn't tell us what effect the whipping had on the woman, but one has to wonder if it did any good. After all, anyone who would set fire to her own wagon probably would not be deterred by a few blows from her husband.

James Marshall

California was in great turmoil in 1844. The people had risen up against Micheltorena, their Governor sent from Mexico City. It was an ill-fated exercise with one very significant result. It denied Pablo Gutierrez the honor of walking onto the pages of history and opened the way for James Marshall to take credit for being the one who first discovered gold in California.

There had never been any love lost between the Californios, as the Mexican natives of California were called, and the governors who were sent north from Mexico City to run the province. By 1844, an armed revolt broke out.

Now it just so happened that in the autumn of that year, Pablo Gutierrez who worked for Captain John Sutter, came into the Fort with some astounding news. He claimed to have discovered gold somewhere in the Sierra Nevada Mountains.

Gutierrez secretly confided in another Sutter employee, John Bidwell, and prepared to show him where he made his find.

Before the pair could leave the fort, however, Sutter received word of the outbreak of hostilities on the coast, so he dispatched Gutierrez to carry word to Governor Micheltoreno that he could count on Sutter. Unfortunately for Pablo, the Captain committed his fealty in writing, and as Gutierrez reached Gilroy, he was captured by the rebel forces. When Sutter's letter to Governor Micheltorena was discovered, Pablo was strung up to the nearest tree.

All the while, John Bidwell waited at Sutter's Fort, unaware of Gutierrez' demise. He had his pick and shovel all packed and was ready to go, until a courier brought the news that Pablo Gutierrez was dead, as was Bidwell's dream of striking it rich. He didn't know where Pablo had found the gold.

Insofar as Governor Micheltoreno packed up and went home, the insurrection was successful. Bidwell, in the meantime, went back to work for John Sutter and forgot about gold until that new carpenter, James Marshall, made his lucky find on the south fork of the American River in 1848.

History well remembers James Marshall for his discovery, but in actuality, had it not been for the political turmoil that preceded that find, today we might be reading how Pablo Gutierrez found the first nugget of California gold.

P.T. Barnum

The name of P.T. Barnum is most often associated with circuses, sideshows, and that famous quote, "There's a sucker born every minute." History, unfortunately, has misdirected this saying. Barnum never did say it. Actually it was coined by his competitor, Mr. George Hull.

Seeing that P.T. Barnum was making a fortune displaying the odd and unusual, in 1868, Hull decided to go him one better. First he extracted a twelve-foot-long slab of gypsum from a quarry in Iowa and then hired a stone cutter to fashion it into a very lifelike giant. Then he took it to the farm house of a cousin and buried it.

When the time was right, Hull directed the cousin to have a well dug at the spot where he had buried the giant. When the well diggers uncovered Hull's giant, they naturally alerted the press. Before the day was out, wagon loads of people were driving out to see the fossilized giant.

Hull, quickly seizing the opportunity, began to charge admission to see his creation. Within a month, the entire nation was reading about the discovery, so Hull upped his price from a quarter a peek to a dollar. That's when P.T. Barnum became interested.

Barnum offered Hull $50,000 dollars for his giant and

was refused. Rather than enter a bidding war, Barnum decided to carve a giant of his own. Within a short time the circus owner unveiled HIS giant and proclaimed that he had bought it from Hull who was now displaying a fake.

Hull brought a law suit against P.T. Barnum for calling his giant a fake, and when reporters asked him about the crowds that were flocking to see Barnum's specimen instead of his own, he replied, "There's a sucker born every minute."

When Hull's case came to court, however, he was tricked into admitting that both giants were fakes. The judge then ruled that Barnum could not be sued for calling Hull's hoax a fake, since it was a fake after all.

So George Hull's name faded into oblivion while P.T. Barnum became known as one of America's greatest showmen--a man who would not only upstage his competitor, but would steal his words as well.

When hostilities at Fort Sumter launched the nation's gruesome Civil War, the young man from Canton, Massachusetts, decided to answer Lincoln's desperate call for volunteers. He joined the Union Army, and in a short time he was helping to guard Washington D.C., a job he took seriously; after all, he had quite a family name to uphold.

On October 21, 1861, his regiment was ordered to Ball's Bluff, just a short way up the Potomac. His job was to rid the area of the concentration of Rebel soldiers that were threatening the capital. He shouldered his rifle with joy; after all, he had quite a family name to uphold.

He engaged the enemy that day and along with 700 other infantrymen, was captured. They marched him to Libby Prison in Richmond, and there they kept him as a prisoner of war. He bore the indignity with honor; after all, he had his family name to uphold.

Then came the order from President Jefferson Davis that some of the prisoners at Libby Prison were to be executed in retaliation for the proposed hanging of a crew of privateers caught in an attempt to run the Yankee blockade. The young soldier drew one of the short straws and prepared to meet his maker, but he did so stoically. After all, he had quite a family name to uphold.

Just as he was on the verge of mounting the scaffold, the soldier received a reprieve. President Lincoln had canceled the hanging of the privateers, so President Davis followed suit with a pardon of his own. Within weeks, the soldier was exchanged and returned to his regiment. His war was a long way from being over, though. After all, there was that family name he had to uphold.

The young soldier fought valiantly during the Peninsula Campaign, at 2nd Bull Run, and Antietam. Then they marched him to Gettysburg. He was helping the wounded after the first bloody day on that battlefield when he was shot in the head and died instantly. Now he wouldn't have to worry about upholding that family name any longer. He had performed after a manner that would have pleased his grandfather. Paul Joseph Revere, Jr., the grandson of that other Paul Revere of the Midnight Ride fame, had acquitted himself admirably. Now he could rest in peace, with his family honor in tact.

Paul Revere's Midnight Ride

Homer Plessy

Any reflection on the civil rights struggle in America quite naturally focuses on Rosa Parks. Her courage in the bus boycott in Birmingham has become a symbol of the entire movement. Ms. Parks, however wasn't the only African-American to refuse to give up a seat on a public conveyance. Homer Plessy did the same thing, but with quite a different outcome.

Homer Plessy lived in New Orleans, Louisiana, during the latter part of the 19th century. He never dreamed that when he got into that ruckus on the street car that his action would set into motion a national policy of legal segregation, nor that the United States Supreme Court would be a party to the injustice.

It was in 1896, that Homer couldn't find a spot in the "colored" section of the New Orleans street car, so he moved on up to the "white" car. It didn't take long for the conductor to stop and have Plessy arrested for violating a state law which prohibited the mixing of the races in public accommodations.

Apparently Homer was not one to give up easily, for he challenged the constitutionality of the state statute. Nevertheless, the lower and appellate courts upheld the law, so Homer continued to push--all the way to the United States Supreme Court, where he was sure he would find a sympathetic ear.

On May 6, 1896, Homer received a stunning rebuke. In an almost unanimous decision, the Court ruled that the law requiring restaurants, hotels, hospitals, and other public accommodations to have separate facilities for Blacks was constitutional. Thus the so-called "separate but equal" doctrine of southern segregationists became the law of the land.

For the next half century, Jim Crow laws, separating Blacks from Whites in every sort of public accommodation proliferated and, every time an objection was raised, someone always pointed to the precedent set in the Plessy case. The Supreme Court had let him down. His vindication would have to come in the person of Rosa Parks who had the same courage as Homer Plessy but lived in a different time.

Rosa Parks

Edith Bolling Wilson

The fight for women's rights seemed to have reached its zenith when the 19th Amendment gave women the right to vote. While feminists all over the country congratulated themselves, there was one woman who was just too busy to join in the revelry. She was already functioning as President of the United States.

The President had been warned not to take the trip. His health was borderline, and he had been pushing himself. Sure enough, as his train neared Kansas, he was seized with a paralyzing stroke, and immediately his entourage headed back to Washington D. C.

While his closest advisors wrung their hands and pondered what to do, the President's wife took charge. No one was allowed to see the Chief Executive without her approval. The President's son-in-law couldn't break through the protective wall erected by the strong-willed woman. Even the Vice President of the United States was ignored by this guardian of the bed chamber.

As for official business, it was up to the President's wife to determine which pieces of legislation were laid before him. Upheld by the warm, firm hand of a woman--the woman who was for all intents and purposes the President--the palsied hand of Woodrow Wilson clung to power. Edith Bolling Wilson had no personal ambitions, but she was determined that as long as her husband was breathing, he would remain the President in word and deed.

With that shaky hand, Wilson signed the few letters and documents placed before him by his wife. Everything likely to disturb his peace of mind was withheld. Even the private secretary refrained from entering the bedchamber except when sent for. He placed his memoranda on vital questions before Mrs. Wilson, leaving it to her do decide when and if they would reach the President. In effect Edith Wilson was the reigning monarch.

So it was in 1920, the year of the 19th Amendment, that Edith Bolling Wilson became, so to speak, not only the secretary to the President and acting Secretary of State. but acting President as well. Susan B. Anthony would have been proud.

Horace Greeley

Horace Greeley, the man who coined the phrase, "Go West, young man; go West," had a lot of irons in the fire. He founded the New York Tribune, devoted himself to the anti-slavery cause, and emersed himself in politics. In fact, he even ran for the U.S. Presidency in 1872, but lost, and it's a good thing for the country that he did.

Greeley had set himself on the path to national prominence by the 1850s. He attended the first organizational meeting of the Republican party in 1856, and supported John C. Fremont, its first Presidential candidate.

Four years later he worked for the election of Abraham Lincoln, but abandoned him in 1864. Greeley supported the impeachment of President Andrew Johnson, and in 1868, campaigned for Ulysses S. Grant. Then the political porridge turned sour.

Grant got caught up in a number of financial scandals, and Greeley grew so disaffected with the Administration that he decided to run for the Presidency himself in 1872, on a "clean the house" platform.

From the start of the campaign, things didn't go well for Greeley. Because he had become the candidate of the Democratic Party, most of his former political cronies were now calling him a fool and a crank. Then on the eve of the election, his wife died. Finally, on election day the voters repudiated Horace Greeley by a huge margin. He was devastated and dreaded the vote of the Electoral College in December, 1872.

Well, that was one indignity he would not have to suffer. On November 29, 1872, Greeley suffered a breakdown of mind and body and died. A few days later the electors met to conduct the REAL election of the President. Sixty-six of them cast their vote for Greeley and thus voted for a dead man!

So it was only through the vigilance of the Grim Reaper in 1872, that a constitutional crises was avoided. It appears the bard might have been right, at least in American politics, when he said, "There is a Divinity that shapes our ends, rough hew them as we will."

Old West Robber

Traveling was never very pleasant in the horse and buggy days. Those ubiquitous highway men who hid in the bushes awaiting their unsuspecting prey made life miserable for everyone and generally had respect for no one. There was one time, however, in 1877, when two outlaws showed that they did have some manners when they bit off just a little more than they could chew.

Under normal conditions, it would have been a nice day for a ride. Constable Harris of Borden, California, had some business to attend to at Big Dry Creek and Millerton on April

25, so he hitched up his horse to a buggy and started off.

As he was driving up the grade from Little Dry Creek, he heard someone shout, "Halt!" When he turned in the direction of the command, he saw that he was covered by two masked men in a small ditch on the side of the road. Both figures wore dusters and brandished cocked revolvers.

The lawman brought his horse to a halt, and the robbers stepped out from their hiding place. They gruffly ordered Harris to the ground, shoved him up against the buggy and disarmed him. Then they demanded his money--all forty-three dollars. That's when they saw his badge. They were holding up an officer of the law.

Well, the fat was in the fire now, and there was no turning back. However, they didn't have to add insult to injury; they could at least show their victim some courtesy.

After rifling his satchel, they neatly replaced all of Harris' official documents. Then respectfully searching the constable they found that he had a pistol. They took out the bullets and returned the empty firearm to the lawman.

Then, as if that wasn't enough, they divided their tobacco with a grateful Harris and even gave him two dollars of his own money, so that he wouldn't be flat broke.

With their business completed, the highwaymen helped the Constable up in his vehicle and bid him adieu. The entire transaction had been accomplished so coolly that Harris was actually impressed. As for the diplomatic thieves, they melted back into the countryside having proved that even a robber could show a little class when the situation called for it.

THE PRAGMATISM OF SITTING BULL

Fate is fickle, no doubt about it. Take the case of old Chief Sitting Bull. He was the magnet that drew all of those hundreds of Indian warriors to meet Custer and his Seventh Cavalry at the Little Big Horn. Immediately after the massacre, he fled to Canada, then he returned to the United States to perform the unthinkable.

The United States was just about to celebrate its 100th birthday when it was shaken from its dogmatic slumbers. Facing an Indian army of over 2,000 warriors, led by Sitting Bull, General George Armstrong Custer and 225 of his cavalry troopers were killed in battle on June 25, 1876.

After the battle, Chief Sitting Bull and his band retreated into Canada, but the government there offered them no succor, so Sitting Bull led his tribe back across the border into the United States. On July 19, 1881, the famous chief surrendered at Fort Buford. It began to look as if his days of freedom were over, then a fellow named Buffalo Bill made him an offer he couldn't refuse.

William F. Cody, for all of his showmanship, was a true western folk hero. He was a scout, a pony express rider, and most significantly an Indian fighter. That's what makes his dealings with Sitting Bull so interesting.

In 1883, Cody conceived of the idea of organizing his famous Wild West Show, and the centerpiece of the attraction was none other than Sitting Bull. The old Chief came out of retirement to perform before crowds in the East. Thousands poured into the arenas to catch a glimpse of the man who beat Custer. Like a sideshow freak, the noble Indian leader was paraded before the audiences to the cheers and jeers of a fickle, white crowd.

The proud Chief remained stoic to the end, but in joining Buffalo Bill's Wild West Show, he revealed to the whole world how pragmatic he really was. Surely, ten years earlier, at the Battle of the Little Big Horn, he never thought that he would be re-enacting that bloodshed before delighted crowds of palefaces. The passage of years can certainly do strange things.

Chief Sitting Bull

The Sultana, a Mississippi River Boat

War often brings out the worst and the best in people. Heroes, cowards, and villains all have played their parts in our nation's conflicts--especially the Civil War. A prime example can be seen in the case of the Sultana, a Mississippi River boat whose greedy captain caused the death of hundreds of Union soldiers.

It was in the dark of the early morning when the Sultana steamed north on the Mississippi River. It had picked up its passengers at Vicksburg and was headed north carrying more than 2,000 men. They had survived the horrors of Confederate prisons and had been paroled. Now they were going home, or so they thought.

Unfortunately, back in Vicksburg the Captain, in an effort to squeeze every dollar he could out of the run, had packed paying civilian customers onto the deck of the ship along with his military consignment of passengers. The overloaded boat pressed on, passing Memphis and continued steaming north until it had gone about 90 miles. Suddenly the boilers exploded. The strain had been just too much. The vessel literally blew apart.

As fate would have it, the levees on both sides of the Mississippi had been so demolished that all of the surrounding bottom lands were flooded to a width of 50 miles. Now more than 2,000 bodies bobbed in that water.

Of that group, 1900 soldiers perished that morning. Corpses were found as far south as Helena, Arkansas. It was America's worst-ever maritime disaster, and it was fraught with irony.

Most of those soldiers had been in Southern prisons for two years or more. After lengthy negotiations they had been repatriated. Families were preparing for their return home. But this was not to be. One greedy Captain and an overworked boiler did what sharp-shooters and prison guards could not. On April 27, 1865--eighteen days AFTER Lee surrendered, the soldiers on the Sultana died with hardly any notice, and that's the clincher. To die in battle is one thing; to die needlessly after the last bullet has been fired is quite another.

Former President Theodore Roosevelt Giving Speech

Although short in stature, Teddy Roosevelt was really a giant of a man. Nothing could stop him when he made up his mind to do something. Take that day in 1912, for instance. Not even a bullet could keep him from finishing a job he had set out to do.

The date was October 12. There was a three way race for the White House, and former President Theodore Roosevelt was on the stump for the Progressives, or the Bull Moose party, as it was popularly known.

Running on the Democratic ticket was the Princeton

professor, Woodrow Wilson, and for the Republicans, the incumbent, William Howard Taft.

The Progressives had moved very quickly to kick off the campaign by putting Roosevelt out on the trail. That's why he was in Milwaukee on that fateful day. On his way to the auditorium, where he was to speak, the former President was shot in the chest by an unknown gunman at close range.

Fortunately for Roosevelt the bullet first went through the thick manuscript he was preparing to speak from, before it struck his metal eyeglass case. The two obstructions reduced the velocity of the bullet before it entered his body.

Doctor's examined T.R. and ordered him to the hospital at once, but he steadfastly refused to be denied his opportunity to speak to the crowd, and proceeded to the rostrum to give the speech with the bullet still in his chest. He began the oration with the following words: "Friends, I shall ask you to be as quiet as possible. I don't know whether you fully understand that I have just been shot, but it takes more than that to kill a Bull Moose."

Well, Roosevelt didn't win the election. Despite this speech, he finished second. Nevertheless, he sure made history. Today it is hard to imagine the kind of tenacity that would keep a candidate pressing flesh with a bullet in his chest.

Mary E. Surratt

The United States was ablaze with fury. An unthinkable conspiracy had unfolded; cowardly killers had struck! People braced for the worst, including germ warfare and poisoned water supplies. Clearly the President had to do something, so he came up with the idea of a military tribunal to try the culprits.

Although these chilling words may have a modern ring to them, they actually describe another crisis our country was facing almost a century and a half ago, and they were the prelude to a judgment that has been debated ever since.

President Abraham Lincoln was hardly cold in his tomb when President Johnson determined not to allow those accused of conspiring to kill him to stand trial in a civilian court. Instead they were compelled by executive order to face a military commission.

A hue and cry arose from some circles as to the legality of such a move. Counsel for the defense claimed that the military had no jurisdiction over civilians, and thus such a trial would be unconstitutional, but in the end it all fell on deaf ears. The President had his way, and eight persons were tried for murder and conspiracy to commit murder.

The military panel, composed of 9 army officers, began

estimony on Friday, May 12, 1865. More than 350
s took the stand, and over the next six weeks a wide
f topics found their way into the official transcripts.
was talk of attempts to poison New York City's water
and to infect clothing with yellow fever and smallpox. In
d, however, it was the assassination of President Lincoln
he attempt upon the life of Secretary of State Seward that
ed the fate of the co-conspirators. Eight were found guilty,
and half were sentenced to die. The other four received prison
sentences of varying lengths.

On July 7, 1865, the four condemned prisoners were led
to the gallows. The knees of one had to be bound for modesty's
sake, for she was a woman, Mary E. Surratt. Within minutes
the quartet dropped into eternity. Not only had the military
tribunal avenged the assassination of President Lincoln, it had
made history by ordering the first execution of a woman in the
United States of America.

The Hanging of Mary E. Surratt

Sam Houston

History has always viewed Sam Houston as a rough and ready frontiersman. He's remembered for his exploits as an adopted warrior of the Cherokee Nation, the liberator of Texas from the oppressive sword of Santa Anna, and the first President of the Lone Star Republic. Throughout his tumultuous career, no one ever thought that Houston would ever have a soft spot in his heart for religion. Little did they know!

In 1850, the Reverend George Washington Baines was installed as pastor of the Independence Baptist Church. Now it just so happened that this cleric, who would one day become the great-grandfather of President Lyndon Baines Johnson, had as one of his parishioners, Mrs. Sam Houston, a most devout woman. At the urging of Mrs. Houston, the Reverend Baines had a number of lengthy discussions with the General concerning his spiritual welfare. At the conclusion of one of these sessions, Houston agreed to be baptized and join the church.

When word got out that Sam Houston had got religion, more than a few were skeptical, and a handful were downright irreverent. On November 19, 1854, the day set aside for the baptism, pranksters filled the makeshift baptistery at Kounty Creek with limbs and other debris. Undaunted, the baptizing party moved to Little Rocky Creek. There Houston made his public statement and ascended from the waters spluttering, "Reverend, you've baptized my pocket book." "Thank God," replied the preacher, "I wish it could have happened to the pocketbook of every Baptist."

According to a church periodical, "the announcement of General Houston's immersion excited the wonder and surprise of many who had supposed that he was "past praying for." The editor of the bulletin went on to state, however, that Houston's conversion, was no marvel to him, for over 3,000 clergymen had been praying for the General because of some of his antics in the United States Senate.

And what was Sam Houston's attitude toward this public reaction to his conversion? It's best summed up in a remark he made to a friend, who upon hearing the news, commented, "Well, General, I hear your sins were washed away the other day." Houston calmly answered with a wry smile, "Yes, that's true. Lord help the fish."

No one can say that folks from Texas don't take their history seriously. Back in 1986, when the Lone Star State was celebrating the Sesquicentennial of the Republic of Texas, officials there tried to retrieve the Mexican flag that had flown over the Alamo in 1836. Needless to say, they didn't have any luck--not even when they tried to trade Santa Anna's leg for it.

As most everyone knows, on March 6, 1836, the Alamo fell to the forces of General Santa Anna. Two years later in a comic opera war with the French at Veracruz, Mexico, known as the "French Pastry War," Santa Anna lost his left leg to a cannonball. The Napoleon of the West was fitted with an artificial leg made of cork.

Then in 1847, during the war with the United States, a contingent of troops from Illinois swooped through and Santa Anna fled, leaving behind his cork leg. Eventually it wound up in the Illinois State Military Museum in Springfield, and that's where it lay practically unnoticed until those folks in Texas asked the Mexican government for the return of the flag that flew over the Alamo.

Mexico took the request under advisement and decided to cooperate IF the Texans would reciprocate. Our neighbors south of the border wanted to have Santa Anna's leg back. In return, they would send the Alamo's flag.

Immediately hopes in Texas soared. and then came crashing down. In spite of all the politicians in Austin could do, nothing could persuade the curator of the Illinois museum to part with the leg.

"We have no intention of giving it up," said Colonel O. Johnson. "There have been several attempts by the Mexican Government to obtain the leg--the last in 1942--but it's still ours." And that was the final word on the matter.

Texas had to celebrate the 150th birthday of the Republic without that famous banner, and the left leg of Generalissimo Antonio Lopez de Santa Anna--the cork one--never made it back to Mexico. Apparently some actions of the past are just not capable of correction.

Generalissimo Antonio Lopez de Santa Anna

Adolf Hitler

In the late 1930s, Americans stood at the crossroads. In Europe, a paper-hanging corporal was mesmerizing Germany. Goosestepping storm troopers marched the streets with arms outstretched in an act of obeisance. Sabers rattled, and America prepared. If only fate had played its trump card when it had the chance, Adolf Hitler might have been laughed off the stage of history instead of terrorizing the world.

The Nazi dictator was the grandson of a wandering miller, Johann Hitler, who plied his trade from village to village in Lower Austria. The elder Hitler lived a rather Bohemian existence, especially when it came to his relations with women, and in late 1836, he took up with a peasant woman from the village of Strones named Maria Anna. On June 7 of the next year, without benefit of clergy, Maria gave birth to a son, whom she named Alois.

Upon assessing his situation, Johann beat a hasty retreat. Alois, meantime, was baptized with his mother's name and raised by his father's brother.

Then, after an absence of 39 years, Johann Hitler reappeared. His brother had died, leaving a small estate, to which Alois would have some claim if he could prove that he was a Hitler.

At the prospect of sharing in his son's inheritance, Johann finally did the right thing. In the presence of three witnesses and a notary, he testified that he was indeed the father of Alois. The parish priest scratched out Alois's last name on the baptismal record and inserted the name Hitler.

From that day forward, Alois never used his mother's name again. Now he was legitimized as Alois Hitler, and when his son Adolf was born, instead of Schicklgruber, He was christened Adolf Hitler.

Had it not been for the tardy action of his grandfather, Adolf Hitler would have been born Adolf Schicklgruber, and that raises an interesting question. Could the Nazi leader have galvanized the masses with the last name of Schicklgruber? There are those who think not.

"Heil Hitler" became the obligatory form of greeting between Germans during the Third Reich. How would the masses have reaacted to a demand for "Heil Schicklgruber?" Perhaps if old Johann Hitler had remained out of sight, the sound of Adolf Schicklgruber would have produced nothing but giggles among the German people.

Fate is fickle, no doubt about it. Take the case of old Chief Sitting Bull. For awhile he was a hero to his own people, but to others he became a pawn. Not even death could preserve his dignity as they refused to allow his dust to settle peacefully.

After defeating Custer in the Battle of the Little Big Horn, Sitting Bull went to Canada for awhile and then returned to the United States to work for Wild Bill Cody in his Wild West Show.

The proud Chief remained stoic to the end, and when he died, they buried him in a rather obscure grave outside Fort Yakes, North Dakota. That's where he remained until one night in 1957, when a group of admirers from Mobridge, South Dakota crossed over in the middle of the night with a back hoe and stole his bones to give him a monument that befit their hero.

After years of ridicule and degradation, it finally appeared that Sitting Bull would be treated with respect. But then the folks in Fort Yakes lobbed a bombshell. They claimed Sitting Bull had never been moved after all! He remained right where he had been buried, at Fort Yakes. The Mobridge people, it seems, hadn't recovered the remains of the great warrior chief at all. What they got were the bones of his horse.

Chief Sitting Bull Monument

President James Buchanan

The American Civil War began under the administration of Abraham Lincoln, or so the history books tell us. We have been taught that the first shots of that terrible conflict were fired on April 12, 1861, when the North attempted to reinforce Fort Sumter in Charleston Harbor. A closer look, however, raises some doubts as to precisely when the War began, and who was President at the time.

With the election of Abraham Lincoln in 1860, South Carolina seceded from the Union and was soon followed by six other Southern States. The fat was in the fire, but it was President James Buchanan who had to cook it, not Abraham Lincoln. The President-elect wouldn't take office until March.

Buchanan would have loved to just let things simmer until the inauguration of the new President, but he was backed into a corner. The recently occupied garrison of Ft. Sumter was badly in need of supplies.

So, in early January, he ordered the Star of the West, a merchant ship to deliver the much needed provisions. Down the coast it went to Charleston. On January 9, it reached its destination. Unfortunately South Carolina was ready.

Buchanan's Secretary of State, John Floyd, a southern sympathizer, had warned the Rebel authorities that the Star of the West was on its way, and a battery of anxious cadets from the Citadel positioned several guns at the shore. When the supply ship entered the harbor they let loose with the first shots of the Civil War, three of which hit the Star of the West.

With that, the Star retreated to open waters and returned to its home port. She had been driven off by hostile fire, but as we said the fat was in the fire.

When Lincoln was sworn in, one of his first acts was to re-order the provisioning of Ft. Sumter. This second attempt was likewise repelled by the Rebels, and there was no turning back. The War may have begun in earnest on April 12, 1861, but the first shots over Ft. Sumter were fired months before, while James Buchanan, not Abraham Lincoln, occupied the White House.

General Lee and Stonewall Jackson

In May of 1863, the Union commander, General Meade with 130,000 men, faced Confederate General Lee and his 60,000 men, along a line south of the Rappahannock River in the vicinity of Chancellorsville, Virginia. Although Lee was badly outnumbered, he did have an advantage. He had Stonewall Jackson--at least for a little while.

Facing heavy odds, Lee took a chance. He sent Jackson with 26,000 men, on a fake retreat. Meade thought for sure he had the Rebels on the run. He was, however, sadly mistaken.

At 5:30, on May 2, Jackson suddenly turned and came out of the woods into which he had retreated. He fell upon the right flank of the Union army and sent them reeling. Then the two armies licked their wounds and prepared for the next day.

On May 3, 1863, the Battle of Chancellorsville was intense. Artillery roared. Muskets fired, and soldiers fell by the hundreds. As night approached, Jackson, accompanied by members of his staff, undertook a reconnaissance of the enemy.

The General started out down a plank road toward the Union lines, but before he did, he gave his pickets an explicit order. Shoot any one who comes up that plank road, and ask

NO questions. The soldiers listened all too well and ultimately obeyed.

Presently Jackson came upon a force of Yankee infantrymen and was forced to turn and skedaddle back along that same plank road, down which he had ridden, apparently forgetting the strict orders he had given his own skirmishers.

As Stonewall approached the Confederate lines, a flash of flame lit the scene for an instant, and within that space of time, in a moment of irony, the South was deprived of one of its greatest military leaders. General Thomas "Stonewall" Jackson had been mortally wounded by his own men, who were simply following their leader's orders.

With Jackson's death, Lee was never quite the same. To have lost his general to a Yankee bullet or artillery shell, would have been one thing, but to lose him to friendly fire was incomprehensible. One has to wonder how things would have turned out if only Jackson had been a bit more cautious in returning to his own lines on that fateful night when he was dispatched by his own soldiers.

Titanic Survivors

It was on April 15, 1912, that the Titanic sank. Over 1200 people lost their lives, but among those who lived was Renee Harris. She was snatched from the icy waters and put safely aboard the Carpathia, her rescue ship, but even then she still had one more ironic hurdle to jump.

The days prior to the sinking had passed all too quickly for Renee. The steamer was making its way at a powerful 24 knots into the iceberg studded waters of the North Atlantic. Finally the unthinkable occurred. The ship hit a mountain of ice, and in about four hours the unsinkable liner was at the bottom of the ocean.

Renee made it to a lifeboat and for hours they rowed. Finally a shout went up. It was a ship, the Carpathia! Renee Harris' ordeal was over--almost.

The survivors were taken aboard and given every

possible consideration. There were, however, limits to the hospitality that even the Carpathia could offer. Once she was aboard the rescue ship, Renee went to the wireless room to send a message to her family. Thinking now that all had been accomplished and turning to leave, Renee heard the operator say, "That will be three dollars please." Shocked, Renee tried to explain that all of her money went down with the Titanic, to which the duty-bound operator replied, "I'm sorry, Madam, but it is impossible to send ANY free messages.

Dumbstruck, Mrs. Harris stumbled back on deck. Then a Mr. Hoyt came to her rescue and gave her the money; Renee returned to the radio room, paid the three dollar fee, and her message was finally sent.

Thus it was that the Carpathia could receive a distress signal from the Titanic--speed through the icy waters at its own peril to rescue the survivors--lodge the poor unfortunates in private quarters--feed and clothe them--provide medical care-- and still refuse to send a free wireless message.

Apparently there were limits to the goodwill that could be offered by the Carpathia, especially when it came to company policy on sending wireless messages. After all, business was business.

Clement L. Vallandigham

Reason sometimes takes a back seat to overwrought emotions during war time. This was especially true during the Civil War. Take the case of Clement L. Vallandigham, a member of Congress from Ohio, for example. That legislator wound up on the wrong side of the law simply because he had the temerity to publicly disagree with the government's war policy. In the end, however, he was no worse for the wear.

General A. E. Burnside, who was in command of the Department of Ohio, proclaimed in a general order, "the habit of declaring sympathies for the enemy will not be allowed." Since it was a well known fact that Congressman Vallandigham was publicly critical of President Lincoln's policies, Burnside put the obstreperous politician in jail.

A military commission found Vallandigham guilty of publicly expressing sympathies for those in arms against the United States and sentenced him to be placed in close confinement for the duration of the war.

When a howl went up over this harsh punishment, the commission shifted its tactics. It reasoned that a more appropriate and palatable sentence might be banishment. The prisoner was taken to the northern edge of the Confederacy and released. Little did the authorities realize that this was like throwing the rabbit into the brier patch.

When the Confederate authorities asked Vallandigham if he was a loyal citizen of the United States, and he answered in the affirmative, they decided they didn't want the Congressman any more than the North did, so they prepared to deport him-- back to Ohio--in a rather round-about way.

The Yankee Congressman was courteously escorted to Wilmington and put aboard a ship, which escaped through the Northern blockade and made it to Canada. Vallandigham, from there descended to his home state of Ohio, where the whole charade had started, and took up right where he left off, criticizing the North for resorting to armed conflict. This time, however, he rattled on unmolested. Apparently his enemies didn't know how to handle a man who just would not remain banished and would not shut up.

President Benjamin Harrison

Every school child knows that California was our country's 31st state, and kids in Delaware know their state was the first. Indeed an important part of the history of every state includes the order in which it entered the Union. That's why teachers scratch their heads when they come to that part of the history of North and South Dakota.

In the beginning, there was no North Dakota nor South Dakota--only Dakota Territory. Then in 1883, they moved the capital from Yankton to Bismarck, and the squabble began. The folks in the southern part of the territory felt cheated, so they applied for statehood, but Congress. turned them down.

The discontent created by the capital shift in 1883, sparked a second, more sophisticated attempt, to create the state of South Dakota out of the southern half of the territory. Voters approved a state constitution and a full slate of officers. The legislature and state officials organized the new state government. Senators were chosen, but once again, Washington refused to grant statehood.

Finally, in 1889, the growing political pressure forced the federal government to act. The Dakota Territory was split in two, and preparations were made to admit the 39th and 40th states of the Union. There was, however, one more thorn in the side of the body politic that would require the wisdom of Solomon. Which one of the new states, North or South Dakota, would be admitted first? Which one would become the 39th state of the Union, and which one the 40th? While the local politicians fought over the dilemma, President Benjamin Harrison came up with the solution.

At the signing of the proclamation admitting the two new states, the President put each document inside identical newspapers. He then shuffled them back and forth until no one could tell which paper held which state's admission papers. Just enough of the statehood documents were left exposed for the President to sign. Harrison put his signature to both documents, and after one final shuffle, they were removed. North Dakota and South Dakota were now states, but because of the President's ingenious shell game, no one will ever know which of the documents was signed first, and folks in the Dakotas will never know whether their state was actually the 39th or 40th to join the Union.

Tecumseh and The Prophet

It is a widely accepted belief among historians that, in describing the past, what people THINK happened is just as important as what really DID happen. No where is this more obvious than in the curse the Prophet placed on the occupants of the White House.

The Prophet together with his twin brother, Tecumseh, were Indian leaders who created a great deal of mischief for the United States Government in that area north of the Ohio River during the early 1800's. So irritating were their exploits that General William Henry Harrison was sent to pacify the Indian brothers and their followers. This he accomplished at the Battle of Tippicanoe, but not before the Prophet pronounced a curse on Harrison.

Nothing much was thought of the Prophet's curse until Harrison was elected President of the United States in the election of 1840. In March of 1841, the 69 year old Indian fighter gave his inaugural speech in a pouring rain, caught pneumonia and died after one month in office. It was at that point that somebody recalled the curse of the Prophet, eyebrows were raised, and speculation ran rampant.

Then when Abraham Lincoln was assassinated, someone remembered the Prophet's curse and noticed something that the two fallen Presidents had in common. They both were elected in a year ending in 0. And when James A. Garfield, elected in 1880, was shot, the curse of the Prophet was given wider credence. What could be more obvious? Fate was decreeing that every President who was elected in a year ending in zero must die in office, and thus it was that every twenty years the curse of the Prophet was renewed. William McKinley, elected in 1900, died in office. Warren Harding, elected in 1920, died in office. Franklin Roosevelt, elected in 1940, died in office. John F. Kennedy, elected in 1960, died in office.

Then came Ronald Reagan, elected in 1980. Would the curse of the Prophet hold true; a lot of folks thought so when he was shot. But Reagan pulled through, thus putting an end to, if not the curse of the prophet, at least the 140 year old macabre belief that a series of strange coincidences were somehow dictated by fate.

James Madison

Washington D.C. is an awe inspiring place. Visitors are struck with the majesty of the city on the Potomac. Little do they know that had it not been for some shenanigans at a dinner party in 1790, The hub of government might have been located somewhere else.

It all began on the morning of July 20, 1790. Secretary of State Thomas Jefferson had come upon a dejected Secretary of the Treasury, Alexander Hamilton, waiting to see the President. Hamilton was despondent because he couldn't persuade Congress to pass his plan for putting the newly created United States on firm financial footing. The obstacle was James Madison, a leader in the House of Representatives, and Hamilton was so frustrated that he was on the verge of tendering his resignation to President Washington.

Although he was not a political ally of Hamilton's,

Jefferson did recognize the need for a sound financial policy, so he offered to mediate the deadlock between Madison and Hamilton. Jefferson offered to host a private dinner party where the two antagonists could meet alone to see if their differences might melt away under the more benign influences of wine and gentlemanly conversation.

Not surprisingly, it was Jefferson who opened the subject, and Madison responded. He objected to the Federal government taking over the Revolutionary War debt of the individual states. His home state of Virginia had already paid off its obligations, while most of the northern states hadn't paid a penny.

At that point, Jefferson unleashed a stroke of genius. The assumption of state debts would be much more palatable to the South if the permanent capital of the nation were to be placed in Virginia. Madison was all ears; indeed, this would stifle much of the southern criticism.

And so it happened. Madison withdrew his adamant opposition to Hamilton's funding bill, and it passed. In its next legislative breath, Congress passed the Residency bill, which placed the nation's capital at its present location on the Potomac.

Thus it was that both the financial fate of the United States and the site of the seat of government were settled at a simple dinner party. As a result we now send our representatives to Washington D.C. instead of Philadelphia or New York, proving once again that politics is the art of the possible.

General Earl Van Dorn

During the Civil War, it wasn't just the privates who died; sometimes the generals gave their lives as well. Consider Albert Sydney Johnston, Stonewall Jackson, or JEB Stuart. They all fell in defense of the South in battle and were mourned by their fellow Confederates. Then along came General Earl Van Dorn. He was shot all right, but not on the battlefield.

Van Dorn was a West Point graduate and career soldier. When the War between the States broke out, he resigned his commission and joined the Confederate Army and was quickly made a general.

His service for the Confederacy was something of a mixed bag. He enjoyed military successes in Texas and in the early defense of Vicksburg, but came out the loser in the Battle of Pea Ridge and at Corinth. Then he found his niche in the cavalry and scored a stunning victory at Holly Springs.

Suddenly Van Dorn was a hero and Jefferson Davis gave him a corps and ordered him to middle Tennessee.

As fate would have it, Van Dorn established his headquarters at the home of one Dr. Aaron White in Spring Hill, Tennessee. Now it just so happened that the other physician in town, Dr. George Peters, who was away serving in the Tennessee State Legislature, had left his beautiful wife Jessie, who was 24 years his junior, at home alone. Somehow Jessie made General Van Dorn's acquaintance and soon was making regular visits to his headquarters. So violently did tongues wag that Van Dorn had to move his headquarters to Martin Cheair's mansion, but it was all to no avail. Everywhere that Earl went, Jesse was sure to follow.

Well, it was just a matter of time until Dr. Peters came home and learned of the alienation of his affections by Van Dorn. Therefore, on May 7, 1863, as the General sat as his desk, Dr. Peters calmly walked past the guards, entered the house and shot Van Dorn in the head from behind. The general lived about four hours and then gave up the ghost.

It seems ironic that Van Dorn would meet such an inglorious end. If only he had heeded an earlier warning from another woman in another town. "Let the women alone until the war is over." Van Dorn replied, "I cannot do that, for it is all I am fighting for." One gets the feeling that perhaps he was talking about more than just preserving the honor of southern womanhood.

Sharkey

Today the name of Wyatt Earp is synonymous with the Old West--you know, highwaymen, shoot-outs, and gunfights on Main Street. But it was only after Earp's death that those stories of his exploits in Wichita, Dodge City, and Tombstone, Arizona, came to the fore. While he was alive, his real claim to fame was a piece of mischief he committed at a boxing match.

San Francisco, California, was the site of the Sharkey-

Fitzimmons fight on December 2, 1896, and it just so happened that Wyatt Earp was on hand for the event. After betting heavily on Sharkey, the underdog, Earp climbed into the ring, for somebody had made him the referee.

Early in the first round, Fitzsimmons threw a punch that knocked his opponent to the floor. It looked like it was all over and Wyatt Earp had lost a bundle of cash. That's when he played his hand. He called Fitzsimmons' punch a foul and awarded the fight to Sharkey!

The furor that rippled through town was every bit as volatile as Earp's Tombstone days. Wyatt faced a bitter public, so bitter that somebody charged the ex-marshal with fixing the fight, and he was hauled into court. The case, however, was dismissed for lack of evidence.

Then a few days later, Wyatt and Sharkey added fuel to the fires of criticism when they strolled into a local saloon together. Ironically, Fitzsimmons was there holding forth at the bar. He was informing the crowd that Wyatt Earp had robbed him of his title, and that if he ever got within punching distance, he would show Earp that a closed fist could move faster than a man could draw a gun.

Sharkey and Wyatt entered the bar just in time to hear the fighter's threats. The room got very quiet and Fitzsimmons suddenly became aware of the man standing shoulder to shoulder with him. He stumbled back a few steps as if he had been struck himself, and hastily retreated from the saloon.

From that point on, Earp's reputation grew but not necessarily as a gunfighter. Until his death in 1929, he was remembered as much for his skill at fixing a fight as he was for settling one.

William Harvey Carney

William Harvey Carney was born in Norfolk, Virginia, in 1840 and attended a school for Blacks which was conducted secretly by a local minister. When the Civil War broke out, Carney made his way to Massachusetts and in time joined the famed Morgan's Guard, which became part of the 54th Massachusetts Infantry Regiment. It was while he was thus engaged in the service of his country that Carney etched an indelible mark for himself in our nation's history.

It was in July of 1863 that Carney found himself engaged in the disastrous battle at Fort Wagner. His regiment was part of a large force whose task it was to storm the sandy beaches of Morris Island, South Carolina and take Fort Wagner. As William and his comrades inched toward the Confederate defenses, the minie balls took their toll, as did the Rebel artillery. Carney was hit twice, but still he moved inexorably toward the enemy. He was determined not to stop until he reached the Rebel ramparts, then he spied the flag.

Carney saw the color bearer receive a hit. It was a

stomach wound, but somehow the soldier held on for a moment. William, who was bleeding himself, reached the mortally wounded soldier as he slumped to the sand. Carney made a dive for the flag. He grabbed Old Glory just before it too hit the ground.

Somehow throughout the remainder of the battle, Carney miraculously held on to the American flag and kept it aloft. One thousand, seven hundred fifty-seven Union soldiers were killed or wounded on the sands before Fort Wagner, and bleeding from his own wounds, Sergeant Carney worked his way to his regimental commander and presented him with the Stars and Stripes. "The old flag never touched the ground," Carney whispered before he fell to the ground unconscious from the loss of blood.

Sergeant William H. Carney recovered from his wounds and in later years was in great demand as a leader of Memorial Day parades and as a speaker at patriotic events. For you see, this refugee from the South, this hero of the 54th Massachusetts Infantry, this African-American who was willing to lay down his life to save the flag, was the first Black soldier in the history of the United States to receive the Congressional Medal of Honor.

Wild Bill Hickok

Wild Bill Hickok! The very mention of the name creates the image of an old west gunfighter. For more than a decade, he made his reputation by dispatching his enemies with his twin colts. Wild Bill defeated every foe. One by one his adversaries fell before him, and Hickok showed no remorse-- until he faced Phil Coe. After he killed Coe, Hickok, weeping unabashedly, vowed never to fight again.

Now, there was never any love lost between Hickok and Coe. For a long time they vied with each other for the affections of Jessie Hazel, the proprietor of a high class bawdy house. In the end, however, Coe won out and decided to celebrate.

Coe and some of his friends went on a shooting spree up the main street of Abilene, Kansas, and Hickok, as marshal, was obliged to stop them. When he was challenged by Wild Bill, Coe made the mistake of drawing his gun. Both men fired twice from about eight feet, Coe missed with both shots, but Hickock put two bullets into the Texan's stomach, and he died two days later.

There can be little doubt that the marshal took some pleasure in shooting Coe, but it proved to be a tragedy in disguise. Just as Hickok was firing at Coe, another man, holding a revolver, rushed toward them. Thinking the intruder was a cohort of Coe's, Wild Bill fired twice more and killed the man. Unfortunately, the victim turned out to be Mike Williams, Hickok's deputy and close friend.

Marshal James Butler Hickok, the stone-cold killer, carried Williams into the Alamo Saloon and laid him on a billiard table. He vowed never to fight again.

Wild Bill was as good as his word, and maybe that's what made him such an easy mark for a neer-do-well like Jack McCall. In the old days he would have been ready, but on August 2, 1876, he wasn't. McCall, anxious to make a reputation for himself, shot Hickok in the back of the head from three feet while he was playing cards in a Deadwood saloon.

It has been said that those who live by the sword, die by the sword, and that appears to be true of Wild Bill Hickok. One has to wonder, however, how it would have all turned out if the gunslinger had not lost a part of himself the night, with his own pistols, he took the life of his very best friend.

Narcissa and Dr. Marcus Whitman

Dr. Marcus Whitman was a New York physician who dedicated his life to missionary work among the Cayuse Indians of old Oregon. He and his wife, Narcissa, lived among the tribe for eleven years, until that measles epidemic hit. When the Doctor couldn't cure the illness, it cost him his life, but it wasn't because he contacted the disease.

Once they were in old Oregon, which included the present day states of Oregon, Washington, and Idaho, the Whitmans built a lean-to mission among the Cayuse Indians near Fort Walla Walla, and attempted, alternating between success and failure, to persuade them to depart from their own culture and adopt a new religion and a new way of life. Then came the crisis of 1847. By then, pioneers were moving into the Northwest by the hundreds, bringing with them diseases previously unknown to the area. One of these maladies was measles, and it promptly decimated large numbers of the Cayuse tribe.

Not surprisingly, the Cayuse correctly made the connection between the presence of the devastating measles epidemic and the influx of Anglo pioneers. They blamed the Whitmans for the hordes of Whites who were invading their lands. By November 29, 1847, 197 Cayuse lives had been taken by measles or dysentery, so the Indians held a council and decided to make their move.

That night Chief Tiloukaikt rapped at the Whitman's door, explaining that he was in need of medicine. The Doctor let the Chief in, as well as a sub-chief, Thomas. While Thomas held Whitman's attention, Tiloukaikt dispatched him with a tomahawk. Then the other doors were opened and the rest of the execution party entered to complete their desired intent.

Before the night was over, ten Whites were killed including Marcus and Narcissa. Their bodies lay where they fell for days until soldiers came and buried them. In 1897, the remains of the Whitmans were disinterred and reburied in a common grave with appropriate ceremonies, and over the new burial site was placed a marble slab dedicated to the memory of the couple who couldn't cure the measles and paid for it with their lives.

Linking the Rails

The nation's attention was riveted on a desolate spot just north of Ogden, Utah on May 10, 1869. For the first time both sides of the continent were being linked. The completion of the first transcontinental railroad was a grand day in American history, in spite of a con-man and his victims.

After the Civil War, two giant railroads, the Central Pacific and the Union Pacific, began a race across the country towards each other, laying track. As the months slipped by, the two competitors drew closer and closer.

Finally by May 1869, it became apparent that the two

companies were going to meet in Utah, so a huge celebration was prepared. Executives from both railroads were present, and it fell to Leland Stanford to drive the final ceremonial golden spike with a silver hammer.

With the crowds pressing and the officials beaming, Stanford grabbed the hammer, while a mysterious person, posing as a San Francisco jeweler, was making his way among the throng.

He passed among the onlookers taking orders for souvenir watch chains which he proposed to make from the golden spikes that were being hammered by Stanford. At five dollars each, the con-man was doing a land office business. Then it was announced that the golden spikes were going to be removed right after the ceremony, so the "jeweler" beat a hasty retreat.

Those who had succumbed to the fanciful oratory of the impostor were livid, and this helps to explain the destruction that occurred after the ceremony. Within hours of the completion of the first transcontinental railroad, those who had been bilked out of their money began to seek compensation, and they got it.

After the two golden spikes were removed by the authorities for safe keeping, under the cover of darkness, the angry victims made off with 12 regular spikes, 6 ties, and 2 pair of rails! In their rage, they had disconnected the railroad link almost as soon as it was completed.

The damage was of course repaired, and neither the con-man nor his victims were ever caught, all of which serves to remind us that very little is sacred when the masses run amuck.

President Zachary Taylor

No one can deny that President Zachary Taylor's life was filled with strange twists. He was late receiving word of his election to the Presidency in 1848, because the official notification came with postage due, and he refused to pay. As a matter of fact, he didn't even vote in that election. It wasn't until he was 62 years of age that he cast his first and last ballot.

The real irony in Taylor's life, however, focused on a controversy surrounding his death--a controversy which wasn't settled until just a few years ago.

On July 4, 1850, President Taylor was attending the groundbreaking ceremonies for the Washington monument. It just so happened that someone passed him a bowl of cherries and milk that warm afternoon, and he became ill. Five days later he was dead.

Immediately rumors began to spread that the President had been poisoned. Southerners distrusted him mightily over the slavery issue, and their criticism was so vitriolic that there were some who steadfastly maintained that "Old Rough and Ready" had been done in with a dose of arsenic.

They buried Taylor in Louisville Kentucky, and as the years passed, the cloud of suspicion continued to linger. Finally in 1991, some historians convinced Taylor's descendants that indeed the President might have suffered arsenic poisoning. As a result, the President's remains were exhumed, and Kentucky's medical examiner brought samples of hair and fingernail tissue to Oak Ridge National Laboratory for study.

Working night and day, the scientists at the laboratory measured the level of arsenic in the hair and fingernail samples. They concluded that the amount of arsenic found was several hundred times less than they would have found if Taylor had died of arsenic poisoning. The President apparently had expired of natural causes.

So Zachary Taylor was returned to his plot in Louisville and laid to rest for a second time. He had served his country one final time by putting an end to rumors that he had been the victim of a well-planned conspiracy. In this case it was fiction that was stranger than truth.

The **Stars and Bars**

The Rebels may have lost the Civil War, but "Dixie" is still being played, and the Confederate battle flags are still flying down South--way, way down South--like in South America.

That's right, the Stars and Bars are still flying in Brazil today as the result of an emigration of thousands of Southern expatriates who journeyed there shortly after their loss in the War of the Rebellion.

Under the leadership of Confederate Colonel William Hutchinson Norris, the Southerners went into self-imposed exile after the War and established a colony called Americana. There they continued their southern way of life, including the preservation of their peculiar institution, slavery, which was not abolished in Brazil until 1888.

The Southern style plantations prospered, and soon a second and third generation of Confederados, as they came to be known in Brazil, replaced those first immigrants. In time nature had its way, and the children and grandchildren of the Southern expatriates intermarried with the general population.

Today thousands of descendants of the Confederados

can be found throughout Brazil, and once a year, they gather to render homage to their Rebel roots.

First they gather at the secluded cemetery in Americana to pay their respects to their southern ancestors. Then they have a party complete with deep-fried chicken and biscuits, corn bread, and candied apples.

There's lots of Dixieland jazz, Southern Belle skirts, and lots of jokes, mostly at the expense of the Yankees. These Brazilian partygoers have names like Jones and Pyle and Steagall, but they all speak Portuguese.

And of course there is the Confederate battle flag. It's everywhere during the fiesta--in the plaza, along the streets, and even painted on the road.

That flag which has caused so much turmoil in the United States, seems not to be mired in controversy in Brazil. Quite the contrary. The Brazilian descendants of the Confederados seem to go out of their way to be seen with it.

So while the South lost the war, it seems that a part of its culture is still very much alive in Brazil, where the descendants of Confederate soldiers love to celebrate their Southern heritage, complete no doubt with an ample supply of mint juleps.

Theodore Judah

The prospects of building a railroad across the continent from the East Coast to California brought the Big Four into being. These high powered entrepreneurs of the Central Pacific Railroad turned a dream into a monopoly, but in the process they discarded the man who came up with the idea.

In 1853, Theodore Judah, an engineer, came to California to supervise the construction of the first railroad on the Pacific Coast. Immediately, Judah saw the possibilities of a transcontinental railroad.

One night in 1860, he held a meeting above a local hardware store in San Francisco and invited Leland Stanford, a wholesale grocer, Charles Crocker, a dry goods dealer, and Mark Hopkins and Collis P. Huntington, partners in the hardware establishment.

Before the meeting was over, the four men had committed themselves to a partnership. Stanford became the president, Huntington, vice-president, and Hopkins, treasurer. The Central Pacific Railroad Company had been formed.

Armed with this financial support, Judah convinced Congress to pass the Pacific Railroad Act of 1862, which provided for generous governmental subsidies for private railroad construction.

The Big Four, as Judah's partners were later called, wanted to build the railroad quickly, regardless of quality, so that they could begin reaping the profits. Judah resisted, so the Big Four offered to buy him out. Theodore snubbed his nose at the greedy foursome and decided to go east once again in search of capital.

Alas, as fate would have it, during the trip across Panama, Judah contracted jungle fever and died. The problem of the recalcitrant engineer had been solved without so much as a turn of the hand by the Big Four.

So the man who dreamed up the idea of a transcontinental railroad wound up on the short end of the stick, just like thousands of other pioneers in California. Small wonder that in the 19th century, folks thought the Big Four were invincible.

Levi Strauss

In the early part of 1850, a young man stepped off the gangplank in San Francisco harbor. He was bound for the gold regions of Northern California. His intentions were to head for Hangtown and there to pan for gold. Instead he struck it rich with a pair of pants, and as a result, his name became a household word.

In the young man's luggage, all that his ticket would allow, were items not usually selected for a gold mining venture. Before leaving New York he had, with the help of his two brothers, gathered a small stock of merchandise composed of heavy canvas and rough materials. This was to be his grubstake. He had figured, rightly so, that goods of this character might bring a fancy price in the West and that he might be able to sell them and obtain enough cash to go into gold mining in a big way.

The man had hardly been ashore a few hours before a passing miner hailed him on the street, asking him what he had in his bundles. Upon hearing his explanation, the miner disgustedly shook his head and said what he should have brought along were men's pants, complaining that the only ones available in the gold fields would not hold up under the hard labors at the mines.

Now the young traveler was not one to pass up an opportunity. He straightway piloted his new friend and first customer to the nearest tailor and told him to make up a pair of pants for each of them from his stock of canvas. The miner was elated with the tough fabric and proudly displayed them among his friends in San Francisco. As the months passed the young man was so busy furnishing material for miner's pants, that his gold mining venture had to be postponed. Everyone wanted a pair of the pants which the tailors were making from his canvas.

And that's how "Levi's" became a tradition in the Old West. Just as western hats invariably became known as "Stetsons" and revolvers as "Colts," so were cowboy pants described by westerners and writers as Levi's, and all because Levi Strauss came to California and mined the miners instead of the mines.

Although there is no hard evidence that Billy the Kid ever made it to California, there is a local legend that insists he once was there. The California yarn centers around an old man who lived in Panamint City in Southern California and was referred to only as the Kid.

The white bearded man was in his eighties, stood about five feet, eight inches tall, and had very small hands. Despite his age, he could whip out a six-shooter and put six bullets in a target with astounding accuracy.

As historian Alton Pryor tells it, the old man was very secretive about his age, and he never discussed Billy the Kid, nor did he ever claim to be the outlaw, but some people did wonder.

Once an acquaintance paid a visit to The Kid in Panamint City and asked him about Bob Ollinger, a bad man in the 1880s who had had some dealings with the real Billy the Kid. Ollinger was known to have been jealous of Billy. Once while Billy was in jail in New Mexico awaiting execution, Ollinger taunted him about how it would feel to hang the next day.

Well, Billy didn't hang. Instead, he got hold of a deputy's gun, killed him, and escaped.

When the old man from Panamint City was asked by his visiting friend if he knew anything about Ollinger, he pulled out his revolver, aimed it at a tin can, and emptied his gun saying, "He's right there where that tin can is a settin!"

The Panamint City Kid fired the revolver six times, causing the can to jump each time. To that, he added, "Take that Bob and to Hades with you."

As both men sat there, the stranger became strangely quiet. The Kid scratched the back of his neck and calmly asked, "Ollinger, did you say? Nope. Don't recollect that I've ever heard of him.

**George Gordon's Mansion
(Today, Leland Stanford Mansion)**

George Gordon was an impeccable promoter. He tried his hand at every conceivable means of making money during the gold rush, and while one of his schemes left something to be desired, a couple of others put him in the history books.

Gordon's first American adventure was to charter a ship to bring gold seekers from the East Coast around the Horn to San Francisco.

He signed up two hundred gold-hungry argonauts for the trip, telling them that they would sail in luxury from New York to California for only one hundred and sixty dollars, a mere pittance when compared with the piles of gold he insisted were to be found in the land of Ophir.

Gordon's luxury liner turned out to be a wreck of a ship with no sleeping accommodations what so ever and very little food. While the passengers were crowded into quarters without bunks, George was traveling overland with more than thirty thousand dollars that the '49ers had paid him for their fare. Needless to say, Gordon wasn't at the wharf to meet his ship. In fact there is no evidence that it ever got to San Francisco at all.

If George was bothered by his con job, it didn't show. Once he got to San Francisco, he set about planning some more elaborate schemes. One concerned a large Mexican land grant on a peninsula just to the south.

The acreage was owned by William Howard. Gordon just knew that the peninsula could be transformed into the fashion center of the West. With the money he made from his transportation venture, Lord George bought some of the land and built a beautiful home.

Later, after California had become a state, one of its Senators purchased Gordon's dream house and the surrounding acreage. The building became the politician's home, and he built a school on the land. That politician was Leland Stanford and the school became Stanford University.

Apparently George knew a good deal when he saw it. It's a pity for him that he didn't keep it.

Leland Stanford

Old West Stagecoach

Charlie Parkhurst was a stagecoach driver in the Old West. Everybody had heard of him, for he was one of the most skilled teamsters around. That's why folks were so shocked when they discovered Charlie's secret in 1868.

Charlie Parkhurst, or One-eyed Charlie, or Cockeyed Charley, as he was variously known, because he had lost an eye when kicked by a horse, quickly became a legend.

He began to earn his reputation when he encountered holdup men along his route. The first time, he threw down his strong box without a single demurrer. The second time, however, it was a different story. He was prepared. As the would-be bandit stepped out into the middle of the road, Charlie aimed a shotgun blast into the chest of the outlaw, whipped his horses into a full gallop, and left the highwayman in the middle of the road.

After that, One-eyed Charlie became known as one of the toughest, roughest, and most daring of the stagecoach drivers in California.

One time while navigating his team around a particularly dusty curve, a passenger asked, "How in the world can you see your way through this dust?"

"I can smell the way," answered Charlie. "Fact is, I've traveled over these mountain roads so often, I can tell where the road is by the sound of the wheels. When they rattle, I'm on hard ground; when they don't rattle, I generally look over the side to see where she's a going."

Charlie continued to whip up a team until his death in 1868, and that's when folks got the surprise of their lives. One can only imagine the shock that reverberated across the countryside when the undertaker informed the people that Charlie wasn't really a man after all.

That rugged stage driver--the one outlaws avoided and fellow drivers saluted was really a woman. All this time he/she had fooled the people with a good disguise, and proved that anything a man could do, she could do better.

Lucky Baldwin

Everybody called the man "Lucky--Lucky Baldwin," but he always insisted that there was no such thing as "luck." He fervently claimed that everything he had achieved was the fruit of his own labor. One has to wonder about that, however, especially when he purchased that San Francisco hotel in 1853.

Baldwin landed in San Francisco with seven thousand dollars in his pocket. Almost immediately he could see there was a lack of living facilities in the city, either for men or their horses. That's why after a few days, he determined to buy the Pacific Temperance Hotel. He was positive that he stood to make good right from the start.

When asked his price, the owner told Baldwin that he would sell for six thousand dollars. Baldwin offered him five. The proprietor then asked, "Supposing I had asked five thousand?"

Baldwin glibly answered, "Then I would have offered you four." After coming to an agreement, Baldwin asked a favor. He wanted to date the bill of sale three days earlier, ostensibly to show the folks back home what a speedy operator he really was. The hotel man agreed to comply.

The document was no sooner signed, however, than Baldwin said, "And now, there is a little matter of three days' board and lodging."

"Oh, yes," said the seller, "You do owe me for three days board and room."

"On the contrary," countered Baldwin. "You owe me. According to this agreement, I have owned this hotel for three days."

We don't know whether Lucky Baldwin ever got the hotel man to pay up, but we do know that a month after he made his purchase, Baldwin sold the property, doubling his money for a profit of five thousand dollars.

After that he moved to Southern California where his streak of luck continued--or maybe it wasn't luck after all. Perhaps Lucky Baldwin simply had a knack for finding those fellows whom P.T. Barnum claimed were born every minute.

Newspaperman Horace Greeley was always taken with the frontier, and he showed it with his now famous admonishment, "Go West, young man, Go West." In 1859, that's exactly what he did, but by the time he reached his destination, he wished that he had stayed at home.

Horace Greeley decided to come to California by stage coach. After crossing the plains and deserts, he reached the Sierra Nevada, and that's where he encountered the incomparable Hank Monk.

Greeley was put aboard Monk's stagecoach, and the driver was ordered to deliver him in Placerville for a 7:00 P.M. speaking engagement. Off dashed the stage with such furious speed and fearful bouncing that Greeley leaned out the window and yelled, "Sir, I don't care if we get there at seven!"

"I got my orders," intoned the driver as he whipped his horses around the spine-tingling curves. In a few minutes Greeley stuck his head out the window again and said, "I don't care if we don't get there at all."

"I got my orders," shouted Hank, driving madly on. At that moment a jarring bump sent Greeley's head crashing through the roof of the coach. "Keep your seat, Mr. Greeley," ordered the unruffled Hank Monk.

Just outside Placerville, a welcoming committee had gathered and planned on stopping the stage to take Greeley and carry him in honor to the city, but Hank had other ideas. He whipped up the team and scattered the crowd with the cry. "I've got my orders!"

So Hank Monk proudly delivered his passenger to Placerville with time, to spare, but it was a rather indecorous arrival for the refined easterner as the stage coach screeched to a stop on Main Street with Greeley's head sticking through the top. The newsman had learned very quickly that no one stood on ceremony when traveling in Hank Monk's stage. It was enough just to get there.

Horace Greeley

Sam Brannan

Everybody remembers Sam Brannan as the man who, in 1848, got on a horse and rode through the streets of San Francisco shouting the news that gold had been discovered on the American River. Few, however, know that Brannan also came within a hair of conquering San Francisco during the war with Mexico. If only his ship had come in just a little bit sooner.

Sam Brannan was a Mormon elder and the leader of the "Water Saints." That is, he was in charge of the 238 souls who chose to go west by sea rather than overland in covered wagons and hand carts.

When their ship, the Brooklyn, put into port at Honolulu, he noticed a number of American warships, including the "Congress." The Saints soon learned from Commodore Robert F. Stockton that the United States was at war with Mexico and would likely seize California. That's when Sam Brannan began to develop a plan of his own.

The Mormon leader purchased and brought on board a hundred and fifty outdated military arms for $3 dollars a piece. He also obtained some blue denim to be made into uniforms and put the women on the ship to work.

By the time that the Brooklyn set sail for California, the would-be warrior was ready. On July 31, 1846, as they passed through the Golden Gate, Brannan ordered all the women and children to go down into the hold for their safety, while the men put on their uniforms. Then he passed out the guns and ammunition. All things were made ready for battle.

Just before he led his conquering army ashore, however, Brannan peered into his telescope, and all his dreams of glory were quickly dashed on the rocks. The American flag was already waving on land. He had arrived too late. California had already been conquered.

Sam Brannan still found his place in the history books. Instead of a great conqueror though, he became the great communicator, as he fearlessly gave out with the shout heard round the world. While the gold that James Marshall found on the American River in 1848 made some people rich, it made Brannan famous.

John C. Fremont

John C. Fremont is a legend in American history, in part because he played such an important role in the drama of conquest in which California was transformed from a province of Mexico into a state of the Union. It seems a shame that the people so quickly forgot.

Fremont led the California Battalion in the war with Mexico and in January of 1847, General Andres Pico surrendered his forces to the great pathfinder. After a short stretch as military governor, however, Fremont got caught in a power struggle between the army and the navy. As a result he was taken back east and court-martialed.

Nevertheless, by 1849, Fremont was back in California mining his rich quartz vein on his Mariposa ranch. Before the year was out, he had been elected, along with William M. Gwin, to represent the new state in the United States Senate, so back to Washington he went. And that's when he got into trouble again.

Before Fremont and Gwin could be seated, they had to draw straws to decide who would get the long term of six years and who would get the short term of just one session. John lost and was destined to serve just 21 days as Senator from California.

At that time, the debate over slavery was raging, and California's two newly elected senators were on opposite sides. Gwin was a former slave owner and proponent of the peculiar institution. Fremont, on the other hand, was adamant in his opposition to human bondage.

Back home, in California, however, the pro-slavery forces were powerful--so powerful that when the 1850 session of Congress was over, they were able to dump John C. Fremont. He made it easy for them. He didn't campaign at all. Rather, he isolated himself on his mining claim in Mariposa and was defeated.

So John C. Fremont, explorer, soldier, and senator, soon found out what every great leader has come to know. The public was fickle, and fame was fleeting, especially in those early days of California statehood.

Chinese Immigrants in California

It was a common belief in California during the 19th century that Chinese immigrants were all addicted to opium. To be sure some of the Chinese did seem to indulge themselves in the habit, but the blame can hardly be placed at their feet. Chinese opium came to America because of the British and their taste for tea.

Actually, the British coveted a number of China's exports, such as its silk, porcelain, and spices, but it was its tea that was particularly sought.

The Chinese, on the other hand, cared for nothing British except their silver, and this of course presented England with a serious balance of trade problem. What could they find to sell the Chinese that would ease the hard currency drain on their treasury?

The answer was opium, a cash crop that flourished in British India. With the aid of some corrupt Chinese officials, a flourishing trade was soon established. British merchant ships traded chests of opium for chests of tea and silk. A number of England's largest family fortunes were soon established in this way, while the Chinese were introduced to opium.

Then came the California gold rush, and the British chickens came home to roost in the hen houses of their American cousins. Chinatowns soon popped up at all the larger diggings, and opium smoking flourished. Just as the Chinese authorities had been powerless to stop the flow of the drug into their country, Americans could only observe its effect in California.

A few grains of Chinese immigrants smoked in a pipe gave the beginner a feeling of euphoria. One pipe per day for ten days was enough for addiction. Once the smoker graduated to three pipes a day, any attempt at withdrawal caused chills, arm and leg cramps, diarrhea and agonizing psychic misery. A moderate smoker able to limit himself to one pipe per day could expect to live another 20 years after his first pipeful.

The heavy smoker of up to eight pipes per day would be dead within six years. Most smokers died by the age of 50, having spent two thirds of their income for opium. These sojourners in a new land definitely paid a high price so that the British could enjoy their cup of tea.

Captain John Sutter

On January 24, 1848, gold was discovered at John Sutter's sawmill on the American River. For a few weeks it remained a secret, but then the word leaked out, and the world rushed in. One would have thought that this would have made Captain Sutter happy. As things turned out, the discovery sent him back to the poor house.

It was money troubles that had driven John Sutter from his native Switzerland in the first place. To escape a debtor's prison, he immigrated to California in 1839. There he was given almost 50,000 acres by the Mexican Governor. Sutter built it into an empire and called it New Helvetia.

Sutter's trapping, agriculture, and cattle raising enterprise prospered beyond belief. In addition, Sutter's Fort became the focal point for the increasing flow of covered wagons bringing settlers from the United States. Everything was coming up roses until he decided to send James Marshall to build that sawmill at Coloma over 150 years ago.

When Marshall discovered gold in the millrace of the sawmill, it was all over for Sutter. The secret soon leaked out, and his own workers abandoned him for the gold fields. Squatters and miners overran his lands, dispersed and slaughtered his cattle, and destroyed his fields. By 1852, New Helvetia was in complete disarray.

Sutter, now hopelessly in debt once more, traveled to Washington D.C. He spent his remaining years pleading with the federal government to compensate him for his loss, but it was all to no avail. His claims were denied, and he died in the poverty that he had tried so hard to escape.

For almost 10 years, Captain John Sutter had been the acknowledged major-domo of the Sacramento Valley, and it must have been truly a bitter pill to swallow when he had the rug jerked out from under him by the discovery of gold.

In retrospect, it is not surprising that he wanted to keep the find a secret--not because he wanted to keep all that gold to himself--no, what he really wanted was a wilderness over which he could rule, and for awhile he had it, until James Marshall came out of the hills with those two little pieces of gold.

Monterey in 1842

The United States officially acquired California from Mexico in February of 1848, but it had had its eye on the province for a long time. In fact 6 years earlier, the American Navy captured the capital, Monterey, much to everyone's chagrin. The entire fiasco turned out to be a comedy of errors--it's just that not very many people were laughing.

In the fall of 1842, the Pacific Ocean was full of warships. Everybody was casting a hungry eye at the weakly held provincial capital of Monterey, and leading the pack was Commodore Thomas Jones of the USS United States. He was under orders that California was not to fall into the hands of any power other than the United States. The problem was that he had to be careful and not start a war with precipitate action. The Commodore couldn't allow the French or the English to beat him to the punch, but neither could he move against Mexico without a good reason. That justification came to him on October 19, 1842.

A rumor reached his flag ship that Mexico and the United States were at war over Texas. "Strike--Strike now," came the advice from his officers, so he struck. At 9:00 the next morning, he sent 150 marines ashore, and they hauled down the Mexican flag and ran up the Stars and Stripes. California now belonged to the United States.

There was, however, a problem. The rumor had no truth. The United States was NOT at war with Mexico, so the Commodore in effect said "Ooops, Sorry, to the Californios, and hurriedly replaced the American standard with the Mexican flag.

Thus, in October of 1842, the United States had possession of California for about 30 hours, until Jones learned of his mistake. The Mexican government was of course angry, and it wasn't until January of 1843 that they formally forgave the Americans--for a price. They demanded $10,000, 80 military uniforms, and a set of instruments from the band on Jones' ship. So in a sense, the short-lived capture of Mexican California by the United States in 1842 was something of a musical comedy.

James P. Beckwourth

James P. Beckwourth was perhaps the best known African-American mountain man to ever hit the West. He stood along side the likes of John C. Fremont, Kit Carson, and Broken Hand Fitzpatrick in the minds of the '49'ers. That's why folks came to Jim when they wanted that Grizzly Bear killed.

James Beckwourth did most of his gold mining near Sonora, but after awhile, he was struck down with inflammatory rheumatism and had to quit. He sold his claim and moved to Greenwood Valley.

Now everybody in Jim's new neighborhood was delighted to see him, for they had a peculiar problem. A Grizzly bear was terrorizing all of the surrounding camps, and nobody wanted to try to take him on, so they called on Beckwourth.

Jim tried to explain that his rheumatism was so bad he could hardly walk much less chase a bear, but his new neighbors wouldn't take no for an answer. They picked Jim up and carried him to the area where the bear was last seen.

Beckwourth hadn't been at his post very long, before he saw the bruin ambling through the woods. He raised his rifle and shouted. The startled bear turned and then charged. Jim's fair weather friends set out in a dead ran and yelled over their shoulders for him to do the same. In their fright they forgot that he could barely walk.

Onward the bear charged while Beckwourth took careful aim. He had time to get off one shot. The ball hit the Grizzly right in the heart, but he kept on coming--for about 15 feet--then he dropped, dead as a doornail.

At the sound of Jim's shot, his neighbors returned just in time to see him hobbling over to the bear. That's when they remembered that they had brought somebody, who was just barely ambulatory, to a bear fight.

Had it been anybody else, they would have hung their heads in shame, but this was James P. Beckwourth, the mountain man. They knew he'd had close calls before, and some of those made this encounter with the Greenwood Valley Grizzly look like a lawn party.

Grizzly Bear

Jefferson Hunt

It was October of 1849, and time was running out for the Jefferson Hunt Wagon Train. They had heard stories of the Donner Party and decided to avoid that fate by heading south from Utah Lake along the eastern side of the Sierra Nevada, into Los Angeles, and then up to the gold fields. As things turned out, they would have been much better off to take their chances against the snow.

It was October 9th when the party headed south, and they would have been all right if only Captain Smith had not convinced most of them to take a short cut through Walker Pass and into the Tulare Valley. Short cuts always sounded good on the trail, so they took it, never knowing what they were about to endure.

In a few days they were facing the wind-blown wastes of a sun-baked desert with mountains all around. They had no choice but to press on.

They abandoned most of their wagons, and packed their belongings on their failing oxen. But without water, their tongues soon were swollen; their lips cracked. The oxen laid down in the sand, never to rise again.

The first to die of thirst was the Rev. Mr. Fish. The next

to go was William Isham, who crawled four miles on his hands and knees in search of water. In camp the men with burnt faces and skeletal frames lay down and waited for death.

By January of 1850, they were emaciated from dysentery and exhaustion. One poor fellow said, "I will just take a little nap" and never woke up.

When the party finally reached the top of the range on the western side of the dreary wasteland, they turned around and surveyed what they had just crossed. They appropriately named it Death Valley, for that was what it was and still is.

What started out as an attempt to avoid the fate of the Donner Party, turned out to be a nightmare of about the same proportions. The only difference was they didn't eat each other.

Death Valley, California

Miners of the California Gold Rush

All kinds of stories of fantastic gold strikes in California in 1848, abound. Tales of miners who uncovered gold by the pound ran rife, and some of them were true. Some of those who were taken with gold fever did get rich. There was however a fairly high price to pay for that good luck.

Old John Cook was an Irish teamster who had been earning five dollars a day driving his freight wagon. When he decided to head for the gold fields, he took out $28,000 from just one spot. One fellow named Hudson got $20,000 near Coloma in only six weeks. A young lad by the name of Davenport found 76 ounces of gold on his first try and then picked up 90 ounces the next day. At Dry Diggings a Mr. Wilson took $2,000 from under his doorstep.

No doubt about it; there was gold in them thar hills, and not a few lucky souls were striking it rich. It didn't take long, however, for these windfalls to dissipate in the heat of human greed.

One freighter now charged $300 to transport three barrels of flour, one barrel of pork, and 200 pounds of smaller merchandise from Sutter's Fort to the diggings--just 50 miles. Pans worth 20 cents soon cost from 8 to 16 dollars. Pills of all kinds, no matter what their purpose, cost a dollar, and shirts sold for $16 dollars.

According to the Rev. Mr. Colton, the Acalde of Monterey who toured the mining area in October, the argonauts paid $400 dollars a barrel for flour, $4 a pound for poor, brown sugar, and $4 for a pound of mediocre coffee. By the fall of 1848, just eight months after James Marshall discovered gold, one had to find an ounce a day just to live, and by that time, very few were still having that kind of luck.

So in the beginning for a few, chasing dreams of golden castles became a reality. For the vast majority, however, wading in the ice cold streams and carrying sand by the ton to the sluice boxes, never did pay off, especially when stories of success drove the price of a breakfast in Coloma to $43, and that was just for a small box of sardines, some cheese, and a little bread and butter.

Trading Vessel in the 1800's

Back in pre-gold rush days, when the hide and tallow trade brought men to California, the captains of the trading vessels had their hands full. Once they arrived, they had to devise some means of keeping their sailors from jumping ship, and that's how a lot of those strange stories about the California Indians got started.

William H. Thomas' ship pulled into San Francisco Bay in 1843 with a load of trading goods. The vessel had not been in the primitive port long before young William spotted a flat boat piloted by ten natives, pulling up along side his ship. In its stern was an imperious looking white man, sitting on a pile of over two hundred hides .

After the man was hauled aboard to parley in private with the captain, the first mate, a Mr. Prentice, gathered his young and impressionable crew around him and told them that they had just met the famous Captain John Sutter, and not to be surprised if the charismatic Swiss tried to lure them off the ship with promises of an unparalleled life of ease at his fort.

He went on to explain that Sutter lived a long way off, up the Sacramento River, and while he had ten thousand Indians under his command, and employed all the white men who came his way, the banks of the river were infested with a cruel and blood-thirsty race of cannibals, who preferred the flesh of an Anglo to that of a bullock.

The mate claimed that these natives murdered and ate all who attempted to join forces with Captain Sutter, and apparently he told his story well, for young William Thomas bought it hook, line, and sinker.

"I believed all that was told me" wrote Thomas, "and [I] helped circulate the report among the rest of the crew."

Captain Sutter remained on board Thomas' ship all night, and then left the next day without so much as a "by your leave." Needless to say, no one left the ship to join him. Mr. Prentice had done his job exceedingly well. How could one accept the hand of someone he thought might eat him at the next bend in the river?

The Phrenologist Defends His Reading

The mid-nineteenth century was a great age for medical quacks, and California certainly had its share during the gold rush. Among the most notorious were the phrenologists who claimed to be able to tell the character of a man by feeling the bumps on his head. Most of the time the public was fairly tolerant, until one pseudo-scientist got a bit too personal in 1850.

When one poor Kentucky farmer went broke in the California gold fields, he turned to practicing phrenology to put some meat with the beans. Every Sunday he would gather the miners around him to feel their heads and postulate on their moral make-up.

At one of these sessions, the crowd was especially large and appeared quite interested. Everybody wanted his cranium examined, including John David Borthwick. When it came his turn, John took off his hat and gave the phrenologist permission to feel his head.

The man gave him a very elaborate synopsis of his character, and if he had left it at that, he would have been home free. At that moment, however, the phrenologist spotted a most interesting specimen, one he couldn't pass up.

He invited the subject to the front, and according to John Borthwick made a fateful miscalculation. Fingering the man's head with vigor, the phrenologist ascribed to his subject a most dreadful character. He called him a liar, a cheat, and a thief. He even went so far as to assert that the man would murder his own father for an ounce of gold if given the chance.

Well, that was a risky assessment, especially in the wild and woolly West. In the twinkling of an eye, the Phrenologist had some peculiar bumps of his own. The indignant miner bloodied the man's nose and blackened his eyes. In short, he got the whipping of his life.

After the would-be scientist received his thrashing, he left California for his old Kentucky home. He might not have made much money there, but at least he could paw his neighbors' head to his heart's content without any fear of retribution.

Pioneers Traveled West in Long Wagon Trains

There were 69 wagons in Edwin Bryant's train, and 67 of them carried women and children. As one of the officers of the company, Bryant was more than a little worried about the safety of the younger travelers. Actually he was afraid of hostile Indians, but there was a more real danger. Those rolling wagon wheels were as dangerous as any Indian arrow.

After Bryant and his group left Independence, Missouri, they traveled northwest, crossing the Big Blue and Kansas Rivers. When they reached the Platte River they headed due west, and that's when tragedy struck. A young lad of about 8 years fell from the side of a loaded wagon, and one of the rear wheels ran over his leg, crushing it to pieces. There being no doctor with the party, Bryant did his best to apply first aid. He bandaged it and put the child in the back of his mother's wagon.

After five or six days, the boy began to scream that he could feel something moving on his injured leg. Upon removing the bandages, the wounds were found to be covered with maggots. There was nothing else to do but amputate. With a wood saw as the only instrument, no one would volunteer to perform the operation, the pleas from the mother notwithstanding. Finally, Bryant stepped forward and grabbed the saw. His gruesome task was hardly half completed when the child fell back in shock and soon died.

They buried the boy beside the trail and ran the wagons back and forth over his grave to keep it safe from predators, and then they went on. Later they would face those Indian arrows that Bryant feared so much, and some of them found their mark. None however scarred the memory of Edwin Bryant as much as the little lad who fell victim to the inexorable roll of wagon wheels moving west.

John C. Fremont

The name of John C. Fremont will forever be linked to the Westward Movement and the conquest of California. The great pathfinder came to the Golden State in 1846, determined to make a name for himself in the upcoming war with Mexico. In the end, he did just that, but not before the Californios made him the laughing stock of the countryside.

Captain Fremont and his party of 60 armed riflemen showed up near Monterey in early 1846. He claimed that he was simply there to make maps of the area and assured the Mexican authorities that he would soon leave, and probably would have done so if he had not been challenged by Manuel Castro. The Mexican commandante ordered Fremont to leave forthwith, and Fremont took umbrage at the ultimatum.

Leading his men to the top of Hawk's Peak in the Gavilan Mountains overlooking San Juan Bautista, he hastily built a little log fort, ran up the American flag, and waited on the enemy. They weren't long in coming.

On March 5, Fremont could see the Mexican army assembling at the foot of the hill. The Captain gave out the orders: "If we are attacked, we will fight to the extremity and refuse quarter. If we are hemmed in, we will die, all of us, under the flag of our country." At face value, it looked as if Fremont was toeing the mark, but when the Mexicans began to advance up the hill, the Captain went to plan B.

After a slight wind came along and blew down the American flag, Fremont took it as an omen and led his men down the escape hatch that existed on the back side of the mountain.

Fremont didn't stop running until he reached the Oregon border, where he learned that a state of war existed between the United States and Mexico. With this knowledge he wheeled around and marched back to Sutter's Fort to assume his legendary role in the conquest of California and to live down the embarassment of having turned tail and run in his first encounter with the Californios.

Slavery

California's first Constitution was written one hundred and fifty years ago, and in it slavery was outlawed in no uncertain terms. It becomes difficult, then, to understand the events that occurred on February 7, 1850, right in the Plaza of San Jose.

The trouble in San Jose began when a white man commenced beating a black man with a stick over the head. The marshal quickly took the white man into custody and along with the black man, headed for the nearest Acalde.

When asked by the pioneer jurist to explain his actions, the white man gave the court a rationale that shocks modern sensibilities.

"That fellow is my slave," said the defendant. I brought him from home with me. When I made up my mind to leave town this evening, he refused to go, so I broke a stick over his head, which I had a right to do. He is my property, and I intend to keep him and give him a good two hundred lashes in the bargain."

The man went on to argue that, although the new Constitution excluded slavery, it did not apply to those who came here before its adoption, and the court agreed with him!

The Acalde considered the case for a moment and then in a decision that was lamented by most everyone in town, he ordered the slave to be put in jail to await his "master's orders" and in the mean time to be flogged publicly for his disobedience.

So the next day, he was taken out to the plaza where he had been beaten over the head with a stick. They stripped him to the waist, tied him up and flogged him. Then they returned him to jail.

The editor of the Alta California expressed outrage at the whole affair and got a writ of Habeas corpus, freeing the black man, but it was too late. By the time it was served, his master had already called for him, and that ended the matter as far as the state was concerned. It didn't, however, end things for the slave. He was still considered chattel property, notwithstanding the freedom clause of the California Constitution.

Biddy Mason

When Robert Smith decided to leave his native Mississippi and join the gold rush to California, he brought his two slaves, Hannah and Biddy and their children with him. Like so many other slave holders, the anti-slavery provisions of the California Constitution were ignored. That's why Biddy took things into her own hands.

When old Master Smith failed to strike it rich in the gold fields of Northern California and didn't do any better when he moved to Southern California, he gathered his slaves together and told them that they would all soon be making their way to Texas. He was leaving the Golden State.

They packed up their belongings and headed out. Their route took them by a resting place in Santa Monica, and it was here that Biddy hatched her plan. She knew that if Smith was successful in his attempt to take them to Texas, she would never be free.

Biddy knew that she had to get word to an officer of the law, so when a Mrs. Rowen wandered into her camp, she managed to convey to the woman that she was a slave whose master was taking her out of the state. The black women pleaded for help, and the chagrined Mrs. Rowen ran to Judge Benjamin Hayes who in turn ordered Smith and his slaves to be brought before his court.

Smith's defense was that he intended to emancipate his slaves once he got them to Texas. Hayes was beside himself and upbraided the slave owner for his deceitful behavior. In a stinging rebuke, Hayes made a point of emphasizing the hypocrisy of Smith's telling his slaves that in Texas, of all places, they would be set free. He went on to say that this hypocrisy was particularly vicious in the case of the children. At the conclusion of the session, Biddy was given her official emancipation papers by the court.

Robert Smith went on to Texas, while Biddy took the last name of Mason and moved to Los Angeles. Not only had she won her freedom, soon she owned a homestead, and in the years that followed she became one of the wealthiest Blacks in Southern California. Biddy Mason's perseverance had not only won her freedom, but it made her a model of the black community as well.

Women--the so-called fairer sex--During the California gold rush, the very sight of one would often be enough to set an entire mining camp into a frenzy, and more often than not, it worked to the distinct advantage of the woman, like that time in the foothills above Sacramento when gender distinctions definitely paid off.

It was just about daybreak when the first miner arose and discovered that some newcomers had arrived during the night. He moseyed down to their wagon, and to his surprise and delight, there was a calico dress hanging on one of the wagon wheels.

The over-joyed miner ran from tent to tent waking up the entire camp and informing them that there was a woman in their midst. Soon every tent was emptied of its inhabitants as a bevy of grizzled miners, shook the sleep out of their eyes to see for themselves.

Sure enough not 100 yards away, there was the prairie schooner with the dress fluttering in the wind, giving it the look of the flagship of femininity. A shout of delight and expectation went up from the crowd of miners and suddenly a man's face appeared through the burlap cover of the wagon. The miners cried in unison, "Fetch her out."

"It is my wife," replied the newcomer. "She is sick--we have been robbed of money, provisions, and everything by the Indians. We want to rest."

"Fetch her out!" insisted the miners. We've got to see her."

"But gentlemen, the poor thing, she..."

"Fetch her out" demanded the miners. So with some trepidation, he did as he was told. When the woman appeared, they sent up three rousing cheers, crowded around and stared at her in disbelief. They listened to her voice and touched her dress and then they collected twenty-five hundred dollars in gold and gave it to the shocked husband.

Then in twos and threes they wandered back to their own

camps, content that they had once more been in the presence of a woman. As for the man and his wife, they departed the next night. After all, there might be other mining camps whose inhabitants were just as desperate for a look at a member of the opposite sex.

A Woman During the California Gold Rush

Judge David S. Terry

Law and order was always difficult to maintain in the olden days--especially in San Francisco. That's why its citizens formed vigilance committees, to take the law into their own hands, and that's why Supreme Court Justice David S. Terry came to San Francisco, to put an end to mob rule. As things turned out, however, he should have stayed at home.

The San Francisco vigilance committees were established ostensibly for "the maintenance of peace and good order of society." In actuality they were nothing more than highly organized groups of mid-19th century minute men--only the enemy was not the British. It was the elected leadership of the town.

In 1856, the Vigilantes served notice on the Sheriff and his deputies that accused prisoners would be held "strictly accountable" for their crimes. The threat came through loud and clear, so the Sheriff appealed to the state. That's when Judge Terry appeared on the scene.

Now Terry had his own problems with law and order. He was generally known to be ready to fight at the drop of a hat. That's what had folks so puzzled when the Judge came to San Francisco to see that the law would prevail in the administration of justice.

It all might have worked out all right if only Terry had not been challenged by a vigilante. The hot-tempered jurist, the law and order man, settled the argument by pulling a knife and slashing his opponent. He was promptly indicted by the vigilance committee for this violent act.

Fortunately Terry's opponent did not die, and he was acquitted of any wrong doing by an official jury. The vigilantes in the meantime gave the judge a wide berth. No one was anxious to take on a proponent of law and order who would just as soon shoot you as look at you.

Judge David S. Terry went back to Sacramento and ironically in 1859 killed United States Senator David Broderick in a duel. For this Supreme Court Justice, insuring domestic tranquillity through law and order meant making the other fellow toe the mark.

Sutter's Mill

California became a part of the United States at the conclusion of the war between the United States and Mexico. On February 2, 1848, officials of the two nations signed the Treaty of Guadalupe Hidalgo, and Mexico relinquished title to California, in exchange for 15 million dollars.

Just nine days earlier, however, a self-employed utility man named James Marshall made a discovery that he tried to keep secret. One has to wonder if the Mexican officials wouldn't have held out for a better deal if only the cat had been let out of the bag a bit sooner?

Marshall was working for Captain John Sutter in 1847, when he was dispatched to build a sawmill on the North Fork of the American River. On January 24, 1848, he found two gold nuggets in the millrace. Excitedly he swore his workers to secrecy while he rode back to Sutter's Fort to consult with the Captain.

When it was determined that the find was actually gold, Sutter also urged secrecy. He didn't want anything to upset the agricultural empire that he had spent ten years building. Sutter reckoned, however, without the industrious Sam Brannan.

Somehow the merchant/newspaperman found out about

Marshall's discovery. Knowing that an influx of gold seekers would benefit his mercantile efforts, he saddled his horse and headed for San Francisco with dust and nuggets in hand and shouting the news of the discovery. Almost overnight, San Francisco was deserted. The rush for gold had begun.

Before the year was out, California had yielded over ten million dollars worth of gold--two-third the price that the United States had to pay for most of the southwest.

So Mexico gave up California for a pittance, and the United States became the beneficiary. One can only wonder how the Treaty of Guadalupe Hidalgo would have been altered if the timing of history had not been on the side of the Americans.

First Gold Found by James Marshall

Nearly every wagon train west had the onerous duty at least once of disposing of the remains of a departed fellow traveler. For overland argonauts, it was rather simple. A hole was dug, the body was committed to the ground, and then the train moved on.

At sea, however, it was quite different, as John Letts discovered on December 6, 1849. The deceased was G.W. Ray, whose intention it had been to return to Maine from California. Needless to say, he didn't make it. He died at 10 in the morning and immediately a gang-plank was made ready. It was hung over the side of the ship, supported by the rail, and a piece of canvas was thrown over it, upon which the body of G.W. Ray was placed. Someone tied a rope around the dead man's waist and then run it down and around his ankles. To that end of the rope was tied a heavy sand bag. Then Mr. Ray was sewn up in the piece of canvas upon which he was resting. Everything was now ready.

The other passengers gathered round and the Captain read a prayer. With the final "amen," the end of the gangplank was ordered raised and down slid the corpse.

In the words of John Letts, "We were under a full press of canvas with an eight-knot breeze as the body passed gently to its watery grave. The last bubble rose to the surface, and the wind passed mournfully through the shrouds, as if sighing his last requiem.

John M. Letts was certainly no stranger to death. He had seen it first hand coming to California. But that first burial at sea was a bit unnerving, even for a California 49'er. Watching Ray's body, tethered to a sand bag, slide down a gang plank and into the sea, was enough to give rise to second thoughts about ocean travel.

Of all of the stories of overland travel during the gold rush, none is more poignant than that of J. Goldsborough Bruff and the time that he had to bury four members of his party. Before he had covered the grave, he was definitely sorry that he ever took the job.

Bruff's company had just reached the Sierra Nevada mountains on October 30, 1849, when they decided to camp for the night. Ormond Alford, his two sons, and their buddy, John Cameron pitched their tent at the base of a huge oak. About one o'clock, a storm blew the tree down, right on top of Alford's tent, killing two of the occupants instantly and mortally wounding the other two.

Captain Bruff was called upon to dig the grave, which he accomplished in short order. He wrapped the corpses in canvas and placed them in the hole. Then he made a marker out of the tail board of a wagon and scratched the following inscription:

"Ormond Alford, 54; and his sons, William, 19, and Lorenzo, 15, and John W. Cameron, aged 22. Killed by the falling of an oak tree upon them, while asleep in their tent, near this spot about 1 A.M. October 31st, 1849."

Just as Bruff was about to fill in the grave, the widow and mother wanted one more look at the deceased, so he jumped down in the hole. "I had a disagreeable task getting down in the grave," wrote Bruff, "treading between their necks, as best I could, and standing in the middle, supporting myself with one hand on the breast of the corpse, while I loosened the sheet and exposed the faces. I then scrambled out and we filled it in."

With his task finished, Bruff then added this appendix to his homemade tombstone: "Their journey is ended, their toils are all past., together they slept, in this false world, their last; They here sleep together, in one grave entombed, Just as they slept on the night they were doomed."

Brigham Young

By 1850, two years after the discovery of gold in Coloma, Northern California had been transformed into a fast-growing, dynamic region. It stood in stark contrast to Southern California, which was characterized by mud huts and a hot, waterless, dusty, near desert climate. Then the Mormons showed up, and all of that changed.

Brigham Young had always wanted a settlement in the vicinity of southern California to support his state of Deseret, so that newly converted Saints arriving from Europe would have some place to gather before beginning the long trek to Salt Lake City. In 1850 he received word that two of his missionaries had found a good spot. The Isaac William's ranch was for sale. They wrote: "Here there is the soil, climate, and water to raise crops of any kind. It is situated within 40 miles of the port of San Pedro and 112 miles of San Diego."

Young appointed two Elders to head an expedition to look the ranch over. He asked for 20 volunteers to go along and got five hundred. Secretly, however, he suspected that many had been lured by the prospect of finding gold.

"I was sick at the sight of so many of the Saints running to California after the gods of this world," said Young, "and I was unable to address them."

So off they went. Their little expedition moved southward toward a little spring called Las Vegas. From there they moved through the Mojave Desert, traveling over a barren and destitute stretch and over a seven thousand-foot mountain range.

When they got to the Williams ranch, the leading elders rejected it, but continued to look around the area. They finally found the place they wanted. The Saints went to work building a split-log fort

There was no government in the area, but the Mormons didn't worry about that. They had brought their own. A ward and a stake were set up, with its bishop and a president, and a high council to serve as a tribunal, and that's how San Bernadino, California was born. Once again the Mormons had opened up and settled a new land.

Aldrich, Lorenzo D. <u>A Journal of the Overland Route to California & the Gold Mines</u>. Los Angeles: Dawson's Book Shop, 1950.

Apostol, Jane. <u>El Alisal, Where History Lingers</u>. Los Angeles: Historical Society of Southern California.

Audubon, John Woodhouse. <u>Audubon's Western Journal, 1849-1850</u>. Tucson, Arizona: The University of Arizona Press, 1984.

Bailey, Thomas A. <u>The American Pageant</u>. Volume I. Boston: D.C. Heath and Company, 1966.

Bailey, Thomas A. <u>The American Pageant</u>. Volume II. Boston: D.C. Heath and Company, 1966.

Bates, Ed Bryant. <u>True Tales of Outlaws & Rogues</u>. Coarsegold, California: .45 Caliber Publishing, 2001.

Berenger, Clara. "The Woman Who Taught Her Children to Be Fools." <u>America: An Illustrated Diary of its Most Exciting Years</u>. Valencia, California: American Family Enterprises, Inc., 1973.

Bernard, Bruce. <u>Century</u>. London: Phaidon Press Limited. 1999.

Bieber, Ralph P. (ed.) The Southwest Historical Series, Vol. VII: <u>Exploring Southwestern Trails 1846-1854</u>. Glendale, California: The Arthur H. Clark Company, 1938.

Bieber, Ralph P. (ed.) The Southwest Historical Series, Vol. XII: <u>Analytical Index</u>. Glendale, California: The

Arthur H. Clark Company, 1943.

Bieber, Ralph P. Southern Trails to California in 1949. Philadelphia: Porcupine Press, 1974.

Billington, Ray Allen. The Far Western Frontier. New York: Harper & Row Publishers, 1956.

Billington, Ray Allen. The Protestant Crusade: 1800-1860. Gloucester, Massachusetts: Holt, Rinehart, & Winston, Inc., 1963.

Billington, Ray Allen. Westward Expansion. New York: The Macmillan Company, 1967.

Botkin, B.A. (ed.). Civil War Treasury of Tales, Legends, & Folklore. New York: Promontory Press, 1960.

Bruff, J. Goldsborough. Gold Rush. Vol II. New York: Columbia University Press, 1944.

Bryant, Edwin. What I Saw in California. Santa Ana, California: The Fine Arts Press, 1936.

Capps, Benjamin. The Great Chiefs. Alexandria, Virginia: Time-Life Books, 1975.

Carruth, Gorton. Encyclopedia of American Facts & Dates. New York: Harper & Row, 1987.

Catton, Bruce. The American Heritage New History of the Civil War. New York: Penguin Books, 1996.

Caughey, John Walton. Gold is the Cornerstone. Berkeley, California: University of California Press, 1948.

Chan, Sucheng. This Bitter-Sweet Soil. Los Angeles: University of California Press, 1986.

Chinn, Thomas W. (ed.) A History of the Chinese in California. San Francisco: Chinese Historical Society of America, 1969.

Clark, Thomas D. Frontier America. New York: Charles Scribner's Sons, 1959.

Cole, Martin and Welcome, Henry (eds.). Don Pio Pico's Historical Narrative. Glendale, California, The Arthur H. Clark Company, 1973.

Constable, George. (ed.). The Trailblazers. Alexandria, Virginia: Time-Life Books, 1973.

Current, Richard N., Freidel Frank, and Williams, T. Harry. American History: A Survey. New York: Alfred A. Knopf, 1967.

Daniels, Jonathan, Daniels. The Devil's Backbone. New York: McGraw-Hill Book Company, 1962.

DeVoto, Bernard. The Year of Decision, 1846. Boston: Little, Brown and Company, 1943.

Dillon, Richard H. The Gila Trail: The Texas Argonauts and the California Gold Rush. Norman, Oklahoma: University of Oklahoma Press, 1984.

Dillon, Richard. Captain John Sutter: Sacramento Valley's Sainted Sinner. Santa Cruz, California: Western Tanager Press, 1967.

Donald, David and Randell, J.G. The Civil War and Reconstruction. Boston: D.C. Heath and Company, 1961.

Dowdey, Clifford and Manarin, Louis H. (eds.). The Wartime Papers of R.E. Lee. Boston: Little, Brown, and Company, 1961.

Drury, Clifford M. Marcus and Narcissa Whitman and the Opening of Old Oregon. Glendale, California: The Arthur H. Clark Company, 1973.

Drury, Clifford M. Marcus Whitman, M.D. Caldwell, Idaho: The Caxton Printers, Ltd., 1937.

Egan, Ferol. The El Dorado Trail. New York: McGraw-Hill Book Company, 1970.

Etter, Patricia. To California on the Southern Route, 1849. Spokane, Washington: The Arthur H. Clark Company, 1998.

Evans, George W.B. Mexican Gold Trail. San Marino, California: The Huntington Library, 1945.

Ferguson, Rebecca N. The Handy History Answer Book. Detroit: The Visible Ink Press, 2000.

Foote, Shelby. The Civil War: Fort Sumter to Perryville. New York: Random House, 1958.

Forbis, William H. The Cowboys. Alexandria, Virginia: Time-Life Books, 1973.

Freehling, William W. The Road to Disunion. New York:

Oxford University Press, 1990.

Garraty, John A. The American Nation. New York: Harper & Row, 1966.

Garrison, Webb. Brady's Civil War. Guilford, Connecticut: The Lyons Press, 2000.

Gillenkirk, Jeff, and Motlow, James. Bitter Melon: Inside America's Last Rural Chinese Town. Berkeley, California: Heydey Books, 1987.

Grant, Ulysses S. Grant. The Civil War Memoirs of Ulysses S. Grant. New York: A Tom Doherty Associates Book, 2002.

Greeley, Horace. An Overland Journey. New York: Alfred A. Knopf, 1964.

Grun, Bernard. The Timetables of History. New York: Simon & Schuster, 1982.

Hafen, Leroy R., Hollon, W. Eugene, and Rister, Carl, Coke. Western America. Englewood Cliffs, New Jersey: Prentice-Hall, Inc., 1970.

Hagerty, Donald J. Desert Dreams: The Art and Life of Maynard Dixon. Layton, Utah: Gibbs-Smith Publisher, 1993.

Hague, Harlan and Langum, David J. Thomas O. Larkin. Norman, Oklahoma, University of Oklahoma Press, 1990.

Handlin, Oscar. America: A History. New York: Holt,

Rinehart and Winston, 1968.

Hardeman, Nicholas Perkins. <u>Wilderness Calling</u>. Knoxville, Tennessee: The University of Tennessee Press, 1977.

Harwell, Richard B. (ed.). <u>The Civil War Reader</u>. New York: Mallard Press, 1957.

Hittell, Theodore. <u>History of California</u>. San Francisco: Pacific Press Publishing House, 1885.

Holbrook, Stewart, H. <u>The Old Post Road</u>. New York: McGraw-Hill Book Company, Inc., 1962.

Holiday. J.S. <u>The World Rushed In</u>. New York: Simon and Schuster, 1981.

Hollon, W. Eugene. <u>Beyond the Cross Timbers</u>. Norman, Oklahoma: University of Oklahoma Press, 1955.

Hollon, W. Eugene. <u>The Southwest: Old and New</u>. New York: Alfred A. Knopf, 1961.

Horsman, Reginald. <u>The Frontier in the Formative Years, 1783-1815</u>. New York: Holt, Rinehart and Winston, 1970.

Hunt, Thomas. <u>Ghost Trails to California</u>. New York: Weathervane Books, 1976.

Johnson, William Weber. <u>The Forty-Niners</u>. Alexandria, Virginia: Time-Life Books, 1974.

Karolevitz, Robert F. <u>Newspapering in the Old West</u>. Seattle, Washington: Superior Publishing Company, 1965.

Klose, Nelson. <u>A Concise Study Guide to the American Frontier</u>. Lincoln, Nebraska: University of Nebraska Press, 1964.

Kowalewski, Michael. (ed.). <u>Gold Rush: A Literary Exploration</u>. Berkeley, California: California Council for the Humanities, 1997.

Lamar, Howard R. (ed.). <u>The Reader's Encyclopedia of the American West</u>. New York: Thomas Y. Crowell Company, 1977.

Lapp, Rudolph M. <u>Blacks in Gold Rush California</u>. New Haven: Yale University Press, 1977.

Latta, Frank F. <u>Joaquin Murrieta and his Horse Gangs</u>. Santa Cruz, California: Bear State Books, 1980.

Levy, JoAnn. <u>They Saw the Elephant</u>. Hamden, Connecticut: Archon Book, 1990.

Lothrop, Gloria Ricci and Nunis, Doyce B. Jr. (eds.) <u>A Guide to the History of California</u>. New York: Greenwood Press, 1989.

Maino Jeannette Gould. <u>Left Hand Turn: A Story of the Donner Party Women</u>. Modesto, California: Dry Creek Books, 1987.

McDonald, Archie P. <u>William Barrett Travis</u>: A Biography. Austin, Texas: Eakin Press, 1995.

McPherson, James M. <u>Battle Cry of Freedom</u>. New York: Ballantine Books, 1988.

Miller Francis Trevelyan. (ed.). <u>The Photographic History of the Civil War in Ten Volumes</u>. New York: The Review of Reviews Co., 1911.

Mitchell, Broadus. <u>Heritage from Hamilton</u>. New York: Columbia University Press, 1957.

Morgan, Ted. <u>Wilderness at Dawn</u>. New York: Simon & Schuster, 1993.

Muir, Andrew Forest. <u>Texas in 1837</u>. Austin: University of Texas Press, 1958.

Myres, Sandra L. (ed.) <u>Ho for California!</u> San Marino, California: Huntington Library, 1980.

Nadeau, Remi. <u>Ghost Towns & Mining Camps of California</u>. Santa Barbara, California: Crest Publishers, 1965.

Nevin, David. <u>The Texans</u>. Alexandria, Virginia: Time-Life Books, 1975.

Nevins, Allan. <u>Fremont: Pathmarker of the West</u>. Lincoln, Nebraska: University of Nebraska Press, 1939.

Newell, Chester. <u>History of the Revolution in Texas</u>. New York: Arno Press, 1973.

Nunis, Doyce B. (ed) <u>The Bidwell-Bartleson Party: 1841 California Emigrant Adventure</u>. Santa Cruz, California: Western Tanager   Press, 1991.

Paul, Rodman. <u>Mining Frontiers of the Far West, 1848-1880</u>. New York: Holt, Rinehart and Winston, 1963.

Pitt, Leonard. The Decline of the Californios. Berkeley: University of California Press, 1966.

Pomeroy, Earl. The Pacific Slope. New York: Alfred A. Knopf, 1966.

Rolle, Andrew F. California: A History. New York, Thomas Y. Crowell Company, 1963.

Rolle, Andrew. John Charles Fremont. Norman, Oklahoma: University of Oklahoma Press, 1991.

Schlesinger, Arthur, M. Jr. The Cycles of American History. Franklin Center, Pennsylvania: The Franklin Library, 1986.

Schlissel, Lillian. Women's Diaries of the Westward Journey. New York: Schocken Books, 1982.

Seagraves, Anne. Soiled Doves: Prostitution in the Early West. Hayden, Idaho: Wesanne Publications, 1994.

Secrest, William B. California Desperadoes. Clovis, California: Word Dancer Press, 2000.

Secrest, William B. Lawmen & Desperadoes. Spokane, Washington: The Arthur H. Clark Company, 1994.

Secrest, William B. Perilous Trails, Dangerous Men. Clovis, California: Word Dancer Press, 2002.

Shirer, William L. The Rise and Fall of the Third Reich. New York: Simon and Schuster, 1960.

Slatta, Richard W. Cowboys of the Americas. New Haven:

Yale University Press, 1990.

Smithwick, Noah. <u>The Evolution of a State or Recollections of Old Texas Days</u>. Austin: University of Texas Press, 1987.

Sosin, Jack M. <u>The Revolutionary Frontier, 1763-1783</u>. New York: Holt, Rinehart, and Winston, 1967.

Steckmesser, Kent Ladd. <u>The Westward Movement: A Short History</u>. New York: McGraw-Hill Book Company, 1969.

Stewart, George R. <u>The California Trail</u>. New York: McGraw-Hill Book Company, Inc., 1962.

Stone, Irving. <u>Clarence Darrow for the Defense</u>. New York: Doubleday and Company, Inc., 1941.

Stone, Irving. <u>From Mud-Flat Cove to Gold to Statehood</u>. Clovis, California: Quill Driver Books, 1999.

Stone, Irving. <u>Men to Match My Mountains</u>. New York: Doubleday & Company, 1956.

Stone, Ted. <u>100 Years of Cowboy Stories</u>. Red Deer, Alberta, Canada: Red Deer College Press, 1994.

Tanner, Ogden. <u>The Ranchers</u>. Alexandria, Virginia: Time-Life Books, 1977.

Trachtman, Paul. <u>The Gunfighters</u>. Alexandria, Virginia: Time-Life Books, 1974.

Turner, Frederick Jackson. <u>The Frontier in American History</u>.

Franklin Center, Pennsylvania: The Franklin Library, 1977.

Turner, Frederick Jackson. The United States 1830-1850. Gloucester, Massachusetts: Peter Smith, 1958.

Wallace, Robert. The Miners. Alexandria, Virginia: Time-Life Books, 1976.

Webb, Walter, Prescott. History as High Adventure. Austin: The Pemberton Press, 1969.

Werner, M. R. "William Jennings Bryan: The Last Battle." America: An Illustrated Diary of its Most Exciting Years. Valencia, California: American Family Enterprises, Inc., 1973.

Wharton, Clarence. History of Fort Bend County. San Antonio, Texas: The Naylor Company, 1939.

Wheat, Frank. California Desert Miracle. San Diego, California: Sunbelt Publications, 1999.

Wheeler, Keith. The Railroaders. Alexandria, Virginia: Time-Life Books, 1973.

Whitsell, Leon O. One Hundred Years of Freemasonry in California. San Francisco: Griffin Brothers, Inc., 1950.

Worcester, Don. Pioneer Trails West. Caldwell, Idaho: The Caxton Printers, Ltd. 1985.

Young, Judy, Dockery and Young, Richard. Outlaw Tales. Little Rock, Arkansas: August House Inc.